FRANKENSTEIN

FROM THE STORY BY
MARY SHELLEY

Retold by John Grant

With introduction and notes by Anthony Marks

Illustrations by Barry Jones

D0510407

First published in 2001 by Usborne Publishing Ltd,
Usborne House, 83-85 Saffron Hill, London
EC1N 8RT, England.
www.usborne.com

A catalogue record for this title is available from
the British Library

Printed in Reading, Berkshire, UK.

Edited by Felicity Brooks & Anthony Marks
Designed by Glen Bird
Cover image by Ian McNee
Cover design by Sonia Dobie
Series editors: Jane Chisholm & Rosie Dickins

JFMAM JASOND/13 00338/06.

ISBN 9780746076651

CONTENTS

ABOUT FRANKENSTEIN

The author of *Frankenstein*, Mary Wollstonecraft Godwin (later Mary Shelley), was the daughter of two English writers. In 1814, at the age of 16, she eloped with the poet Percy Bysshe Shelley, whom she later married. They journeyed through France and Italy, and in 1816 settled near Geneva, Switzerland. Her step-sister Claire also lived with them, and the poet Byron lived nearby. Mary Shelley later described that period as "a wet, ungenial summer" and wrote that because of the endless rain, they were often unable to leave the house for several days. To amuse themselves, they read to each other from books of French and German ghost stories until, one day, Byron suggested that they each write a ghost story instead. While the others quickly gave up, Mary Shelley persisted. She later developed her story into the novel *Frankenstein*, which was published in 1818 when she was just 21 years old. It was an instant success, and is now one of the most famous novels ever written in the English language.

In her introduction to a new edition of the novel in 1831, Mary Shelley described how the idea for the story came to her one night as she lay in bed. She had spent the evening discussing current developments in science and philosophy with Shelley and Byron. (This was an age of rapid scientific discovery, and they were well aware of, for example, Volta's and Galvani's experiments with electricity, as well as the work of Humphry Davy on oxygen.) They were considering how electricity could be used to reanimate a corpse, or the possibility of creating a living being out of dead body parts. These ideas took hold in her imagination in the form of Victor Frankenstein.

In the original publication, *Frankenstein* has a subtitle: "The Modern Prometheus". This refers to an ancient Greek myth about Prometheus, a man who brought fire from the realm of the gods to humans on earth. A lesser-known version of the myth refers to Prometheus creating human life out of a clay model. This myth is also referred to in poetry written by Shelley and Byron written around this time. Mary Shelley's creation is a modern fusion of these two myths, for Victor Frankenstein uses electricity to animate human flesh. And like the ancient Prometheus, who was punished by the gods for his arrogance, Frankenstein lived to regret his deeds.

Frankenstein has fascinated readers for nearly two centuries. There are several reasons for this. Firstly, while it is horrific, it is not just a horror story. It also asks questions about the purpose of science and the responsibilities of scientists. The author seems to find the power to create life exciting and terrifying at the same time: Victor is both fascinated and repelled by what he has done. Secondly, the book asks whether people are born good, evil or neutral. (This was a popular philosophical question at the time the book was written and it continues to provoke discussion today.) Frankenstein's monster cannot tell good from evil, but he learns to become evil because he is badly treated, first by Frankenstein himself, then by other people in society. But as his understanding grows, the monster learns that evil is wrong. This is a third strand of the book, which deals with the power of learning and education.

Frankenstein provoked very strong reactions. For example William Beckford, himself a writer of horror and fantasy books, called it "the foulest Toadstool that has yet sprung up from the reeking dunghill of the present times". But these reactions only contributed to the book's fame. Mary Shelley was also surprised and slightly scared by the success of her book. She likened her "creation" to Frankenstein's monster, but unlike Victor, she was happy to wish it well. In her introduction to the 1931 edition she wrote, "I bid my hideous progeny go forth and prosper". Her inspiration ensured that people would keep returning to her work again and again, to be both frightened and fascinated.

ICEBOUND

High above the Arctic Circle, in the Land of the
Midnight Sun, Captain Walton, polar explorer, peered
through the steam of his breath at the thin channel of
black water ahead of him. Shivering, he pulled the
thick hood of his fur overcoat closer around his head
and stamped his feet on the deck. Then he squinted
for the thousandth time at the orange sun, low in the
sky. He looked back to the channel: narrow as it was,

it seemed to get even narrower in the distance. Then another gust of fog swept across his gaze, and behind it came billows of snow. What had been a sort of twilight deepened into a misty darkness.

Reluctantly, he turned to his first mate, Rostop.

"We'll have to lay anchor," he said. "Give the command to the men. We can't continue in these conditions." The huge man looked equally reluctant, but after a moment shrugged philosophically.

"Yes, Cap'n," he said.

For many weeks now Walton's little ship, the *Margaret Saville*, had been working its way through the unexplored polar wastes, heading for the North Pole. Much of the time had been spent in perpetual dusk, but in another few weeks a six-month darkness would fall.

Walton shivered again. Perhaps they had enough food and fuel aboard to survive the winter months should they be caught in the ice, but he was uncertain. Though his every instinct cried out against it, he knew that if the weather got worse he would have to turn the *Margaret Saville* around and head south. Maybe he could mount another expedition next year, but he doubted whether he had the funds to finance it. He crossed his fingers and stared out into the fog and swirling snow, praying that they would disappear as quickly as they had descended on the little vessel.

Rostop turned away, then paused.

"Hear that, Cap'n?" he said.

"Hear what?" Rostop gestured vaguely at the white

blankness surrounding them.

"Out there," he said. "Bells. Dogs."

Walton listened carefully. At first he could detect nothing, but after a while a muffled sound began to reach his ears. Just at that moment an eddy of the whistling wind cleared the mist and snow away, and far in the distance he could see a black shape moving swiftly against the white plains of ice.

"Quick, Rostop!" he snapped. "Pass me the telescope!"

With the telescope to his eye he could make out a sled being pulled rapidly across the ice by a team of huskies. As the driver raised his whip to encourage the dogs to go even faster, Walton's attention was drawn to him.

"A giant," he breathed. "Even bigger than you are, Rostop. Here, take a look." He passed over the telescope and wiped the back of his glove across his beard, trying to clear it of ice. After a moment the first mate hissed, but made no further comment.

"Let's hope there aren't too many more of those roaming the polar wastes," said Walton, trying to sound nonchalant. "We'll be in for a fine time if there are, eh, Rostop?"

"He'd have us for dinner," said the mate.

The fog and the blizzard returned and, after the ship had been firmly secured to the ice, Walton ordered rum to be brought out to go with their supper. When he and the crew had eaten, they retired to their bunks, hearing the creaking of the ice all around as they tried to sleep.

Walton awoke to the sound of shouting voices. While groping around for his clothes, he tried to make sense of what was being said. But it was only when he came up on deck that he could make out some of the words. Two or three of his crew were leaning over the rails, calling. He hurried forward to join them. At last the storm had abated, and the ice had broken away from around the *Margaret Saville*. The ship, still moored to the ice, was bobbing in the water.

As Walton had slept, the ice had ripped itself apart. The far shore seemed distant.

Between the ship and the shore, however, there was a floating island of ice. On it there was a man with a dog sled, looking in the direction of the ship and waving his hands above his head. Around him lay the stiffened bodies of the dogs of his team; only one still seemed to be alive. For a moment the captain thought this must be the giant he had seen through the telescope the night before, but then he realized it was merely a normal man. He was shouting in a language Walton did not understand.

"What's he saying?" Walton asked the crewman next to him. "Do you know?"

"He wants to know whether we are bound north or south."

"With the weather like this," said Walton, "I hardly care to guess. But I want to continue heading north. Tell him that."

The crewman cupped his hands to his mouth and bellowed out some staccato syllables which Walton vaguely recognized as German. But he understood the distant figure's reply pefectly. For this time he spoke in English, though with a curious inflection.

"Your captain," the stranger shouted across the ice, "he is English?"

"Yes," Walton yelled back. "I'm English."

A whim of the current brought the island of ice closer to the *Margaret Saville*.

"If you're indeed heading north," shouted the stranger, "then for God's sake let me come aboard!"

With difficulty the crew managed to haul the man over the rail and onto the deck. Rostop rescued the dog as well, and it whimpered appreciatively alongside his knee as he scraped his gloved fingers over its forehead and tugged its ears.

"Quick!" said Walton sharply. "Get this poor man below! Put him in my bunk. Heat up some soup."

The stranger, on his hands and knees, looked up at Walton from the deck. The captain thought he had never seen a pair of eyes so weary, and yet there was a fire of fury burning in them.

"You are kind," said the man in his slightly stilted English. He was wearing furs much like those of Walton and the rest of the crew. "I have not eaten for days. When the dogs died I almost. . ." He paused, and Walton thought he heard the beginning of a sob.

"You have earned the thanks of Victor Frankenstein," concluded the man after a while, allowing Rostop to put a blanket around him and then pick him up bodily.

"Of Victor Frankenstein," repeated the stranger as Rostop carried him to Walton's cabin, the husky trotting along behind. Walton stared after him. Unnoticed, the rift between the shores of ice began to narrow once more.

"I have a story to tell." began Frankenstein as Rostop tucked the blankets around him. "I must tell it before I die."

"I'm sure it's a fine story," said Rostop, trying to make his gruff voice sound soothing, "but it can wait until morning."

The stranger grabbed his arm. "No! You don't understand! It's a story I have to tell!"

Rostop raised a bushy eyebrow.

"There are stories I could tell you," he said, "but you'd probably not want to hear them. In Riga, for example, there was this – "

"Please," begged Frankenstein. "Sit down beside me and listen."

"Let the man speak," said Walton quietly from the cabin door. The first mate grunted.

"All of you! I must tell all of you!"

Walton shrugged. There wasn't much else for the crew to do at the moment. Perhaps it would even be a good story. He turned and called over his shoulder for the other men to come below.

Once they were all in the cabin there was little room left for comfort, but after the first few minutes of the stranger's story none of them noticed that.

"I was leaving home to attend the university in Ingolstadt," he began. "Elizabeth was there, telling me to be careful. . ."

Hours later, when he fell asleep, his story only part-told, they left his bedside to discover that the *Margaret Saville* was locked fast in the ice.

To Create Life

"You will be careful, won't you?" said Elizabeth plaintively, staring up at Victor. He had never seen her look so pretty, although there were tears in her eyes. In the background Victor's father was openly weeping at the prospect of his son's departure. William, Victor's younger brother by seven years, was striving manfully to keep his eyes dry as he clung to the waist of his nanny, Justine Moritz.

Beside him in the carriage, Victor's best friend Henry Clerval stirred restlessly, eager that the two of them should be on their way to Ingolstadt, but too courteous to say so. One of the horses whinnied. Victor reached down through the window and tousled Elizabeth's fair hair. The wind was catching her curls and making them flutter around her face.

"Of course I'll be careful," he said, forcing his voice to stay light. "The university is a safe enough place. Besides, I'll have Henry here" – he nudged his friend in the ribs – "to look after me and keep me in line!"

Henry laughed. Like Victor he was seventeen. The two had been friends since boyhood. Elizabeth was a year younger. As children the three of them had played together in the fields surrounding the Frankenstein estate on the outskirts of Geneva, where the tall Swiss mountains looked down austerely on their games.

Then, a few years ago, Victor's father – whom Elizabeth also called 'father', though in fact the girl was adopted – had decreed that from now on Elizabeth must be groomed for ladyhood. And it was then Henry had begun to realize, from the way Victor and Elizabeth occasionally looked at each other, that there was a special bond between his two friends, a bond which had grown ever stronger as they reached adulthood.

Elizabeth made a strained attempt at a smile, her eyes still locked on Victor's.

"But it will be many years before we see you again," she said.

Justine, a few yards away, let out a wail. William buried his face in her dress. Although, as a nanny, Justine was officially a servant, she had become more like an elder sister to the boy. She had come from a poor family and had been employed by Baron Frankenstein almost as an act of charity, but now it was difficult for any of the Frankensteins to imagine their family without her.

"Not so many years," said Victor quietly to Elizabeth. "The time will pass more quickly than a long, tearful farewell." Elizabeth nodded, understanding. She took his hand and brushed a kiss across the back of his fingers.

"I'll be thinking about you every minute of every day of every one of those years," she murmured.

Victor lowered his eyes.

"And I'll be thinking of you too," he said slowly. "I wish . . ." He paused, glancing at the impatient horses. He cleared his throat.

"I'll come home for holidays whenever I can."

Elizabeth took a couple of paces away, and Henry shouted to the coachman to drive on. Within moments, when Victor looked back as the carriage rounded a curve in the long driveway, Elizabeth was a mere dash of blue in front of the gaunt stone façade of Castle Frankenstein, but through the tears in his eyes he could see that she was still waving.

As they neared Ingolstadt, ten days later, the two young men leaned forward intently in their seats, hoping to catch their first glimpse of the German university town in which they were to spend the next few years. Henry planned to study the classical languages, but Victor was intent on the sciences – in particular, the biological and medical sciences. He couldn't remember when he'd first had the ambition to help the sick and suffering in the world; it had been a part of him for so long that he'd forgotten it not being there.

Now the excitement of reaching the university – where he would be allowed to continue his fumbling schoolboy experiments – was so great that he felt he could hardly breathe.

"There!" said Henry, pointing.

Victor followed the direction of Henry's finger, and sure enough could see a church spire.

"At last," he said, pulling at his friend's shoulder so he could get a better view. He wanted to shout at the coachman to make the horses go faster, but realized it would be useless. The road they were on was rutted and irregular, and he and Henry were being bounced from side to side.

They came around the shoulder of a gently sloping hill and there, laid out in the valley below them, was the town of Ingolstadt. Henry let out an enthusiastic whoop of joy.

The university town looked beautiful in the early evening light. Already there were lamps burning at some of the windows. As they drew nearer, the carriage speeding down the long, well-surfaced road that led to Ingolstadt, Victor could see the many churches as well as the buildings that housed the university. Huddled around these larger edifices were countless smaller ones: houses with roofs of stone or thatch, gabled inns, schools, a place that looked like a kindergarten, and brightly-lit shops with bowed windows made of dozens of hand-sized panes of glass. It all seemed so terribly different from Geneva – so much more sophisticated.

Victor smiled to himself. In fact Ingolstadt was not really unlike Geneva at all. It was simply that the town held the university – the goal he'd been striving to reach since he first became intrigued by, and then obsessed by, the sciences.

It took the coachman almost an hour to find the lodgings that had been booked for Henry. After searching among the higgledy-piggledy streets, they finally drew up in front of a rather forbidding ramshackle house. Henry was first to climb down, and Victor and the coachman helped him struggle with his luggage up some narrow, crooked stairs to a cramped little room. Henry's landlady, a dour widow in black clothing, looked on morosely as Henry threw himself down on the bed.

"I'll see you in the morning, Victor," he said cheerfully, "assuming I wake up before the afternoon."

"Not tomorrow," replied Victor, pausing in the doorway. He patted his pocket. His father had given him letters of introduction to some of the leading professors at the university. To Victor they were more valuable than gold. "I don't want to wait a day before I find someone who will let me study under him."

"You take life so seriously," laughed Henry.

"How very true," mumbled Victor to himself as he followed the coachman back down the rickety stairs. "But in quite a different way than you think."

Professor Krempe was the first scholar Victor called on the next morning, and within minutes he wished that he hadn't. The professor was a squat man, yet somehow seemed much larger despite the fact that his shoulders slumped habitually forward so that his eyes appeared always to be staring at and despising everything they saw. He had long, greasy black hair, but not quite enough of it, so his white scalp showed through in unexpected places.

"So, my fine young man from Geneva," he said with a sneer. "What have you learned of the sciences so far that you think it would be worth my while trying to teach you more?"

"Albertus Magnus," said Victor, trying not to quail under Professor Krempe's stare. "And Paracelsus." He waved a hand. "All the greatest scientists."

"Alchemists!" barked the Professor. He slammed his fist on his desk so that the inkwells rattled. "Buffoons! Fools who thought they could turn iron into gold!"

"But –" Victor began.

"Silence!"

Then Professor Krempe's mood changed. "I suppose it's only to be expected," he said, a bit more gently. "In Geneva there'd be no one to tell you any better." He twisted in his chair and glared out through the window at the Cathedral of San Sebastian on the far side of the square. "It's to your credit, young man, that you were interested enough in science to force yourself to read such twaddle."

"I didn't force myself," said Victor. "I was fascinated –"

"Silence!" Professor Krempe suddenly shouted again. He hit the desk even harder than before, but this time he didn't look around at Victor. "I'm not interested in your delusions. What intrigues me more is your enthusiasm. Hmm . . ."

He spun his chair around, then rested his chin on his knuckles for a while. Victor fidgeted nervously.

"Yes," said Professor Krempe at last, "I feel you may have something of what I require in my students. You've been exploring a blind alley in your studies so far, young –" Professor Krempe scrabbled on his desk for the letter of introduction "– young Frankenstein, but you have the thirst for discovery which every true scientist needs. I think I will take you on."

Abruptly he smiled. It was not a pretty sight.

"Consider yourself lucky, Master Frankenstein," he said. "Forty-nine out of every fifty would-be students who come to me are turned away, because all they want me to do is give them the knowledge that I have. You, though – you, I suspect, will not be satisfied until you know more than I do."

Victor made a noncommittal noise. Professor Krempe continued to stare at him.

"It's true," Victor managed to say at last. "I want – I need – to find out things that no one else knows."

"Well, young man," said Professor Krempe decisively, "that's settled, then. You will study physics with me each morning on Mondays, Wednesdays and Fridays, and on Tuesdays, Thursdays and Saturdays your tutor shall be Professor Waldman, who will educate you in chemistry. The Sabbath you will of course reserve for your devotions."

"But I wanted to study medi-" said Victor hopelessly.

"Medicine and biology are nothing more than physics and chemistry," said Professor Krempe with a derisive snort.

He was scribbling on a sheet of paper. Once finished, he blew on the ink and passed the paper over to Victor. "I ask one more promise of you. Tonight you will make a bonfire of all your books by Cornelius Agrippa and Albertus Magnus and every other fraud who claimed they would discover the impossible. If nothing else, the flames will keep you warm. And tomorrow you'll buy yourself the books I've listed here. You do have enough money, don't you?" He looked across at Victor with a cocked eyebrow.

Victor nodded.

"Good," said Professor Krempe, dismissing him with a flick of his hand. "So many of your fellow students have no money at all, and I get tired of buying books for them."

Over the next two years Victor threw himself into his studies with an enthusiasm that astonished both his fellow students and Professor Waldman, the mild-mannered man who gently encouraged Victor's experiments in chemistry. Victor saw Henry occasionally, but less and less as their different interests drew them apart.

Professor Krempe watched everything with a sarcastic grin, and was generally abrupt and rude to Victor, often reminding him of the days when he had believed that the works of Paracelsus were the last word in science. Yet it was Professor Krempe to whom Victor more often turned when baffled by a problem, and sometimes they would talk over scientific matters far into the night, sitting comfortably across from each other at Professor Krempe's fireside and sipping Professor Krempe's brandy.

It was on one of these nights that Victor plucked up the courage to broach something that had been worrying him.

"Cornelius Agrippa and the other alchemists were not totally wrong about everything," he said nervously, aware that he had had just a little too much brandy. It was a grim winter's night and rain pelted the windows. "You and Professor Waldman have taught me that the body is nothing but a machine. You say that it's just a collection of levers and chemical reactions. But surely it's much more than that.

Without something extra it would be just dead matter . . . or" – Victor was warming to his theme – "even if it could move around, it wouldn't be able to think. It wouldn't be able to talk things over the way we're talking things over now."

Professor Krempe grunted. In the light from the hearth his probing eyes glowed red.

"And what would you say this 'something extra' might be?" he said, as if ready either to laugh at Victor or throw him out into the night. "The soul?"

"No," said Victor firmly. "I can't believe there's any such thing as the soul. We're modern men of science" – Professor Krempe's lips, unnoticed by his young companion, curled into a smile – "and we're used to finding things, and measuring them. But no one has yet detected even the faintest whiff of a soul."

"No one has ever tracked down the home of the mind," said Professor Krempe softly, "but I'm sure you'll agree that each of us has a mind."

The windows suddenly lit up, and a few instants later there was a crash of thunder from outside.

"That's . . . that's different," said Victor irritably. "Each Sunday I go to San Sebastian to pray for the good of my soul, but I really don't know what I'm praying for."

Professor Krempe said nothing.

"It's not that I don't believe in God . . ." started Victor, but then he stopped. Did he really believe in God, or had he lost his faith over the past two years? The brandy made him shy away from the question.

"I believe in God," said Professor Krempe after a

long pause. Lightning flashed again, and Victor leaned forward to hear the professor's words over the loud thunder. "But I believe, too," he continued, "that God gave us free will. If you can find the secret of the soul, my proud young baron-to-be, you will have found the secret of life. And, if you can find the secret of life and discover that it is not the soul . . ."

He let the words hang in the air.

A seam of resin in the firewood suddenly popped, distracting them both. Professor Krempe stretched out a leg and stamped out a spark that had landed on the hearthrug. "A final brandy?" he said.

26

"No," said Victor, looking out of the window. "The weather looks as if it's getting worse. I'd better go. Anyway, I think I've had enough already."

As he walked back to his lodgings through the thunderstorm, his shoulders hunched against the driving rain, he watched the lightning and thought more about the mysterious force that turned the machine that was the body into a thinking being. He had heard from Professor Waldman about the experiments the Italian scientist Luigi Galvani had carried out not long ago, making a dead frog twitch by applying an electric current. "Animal electricity" was what Galvani had called the force responsible for the twitch. A further flash of lightning seemed to split the heavens wide open.

If a small jolt of current could make a frog twitch, what might the power of a bolt of lightning do to a human corpse? Could the electricity animate not just the body but the mind? No, of course not – that was a crazy idea. Surely. He had had too much of Krempe's brandy. But if one could grow a person from living tissue . . .

The body was made from cells, and the brain was a part of the body. It, too, was made up of cells. Were all the secrets of the brain's cells locked up in those of the muscles, or the heart, or . . . ?

He trudged slowly on to his lodgings through the rain, ideas and possibilities flashing through his mind like the lightning in the sky.

He had planned to go back to Geneva the next summer, but somehow there just never seemed to be time. On one of the rare occasions he saw Henry he asked his friend to give his regards to Elizabeth – " I would, anyway," said Henry. Victor also gave Henry a sealed packet containing a long and effusive love letter to her. During the times when he wasn't working – and these were becoming increasingly rare – Victor missed Elizabeth more than he could have imagined.

"Are you all right?" said Henry, staring at Victor's pale face, red-rimmed eyes and unshaven chin as they stood in the street outside Victor's lodgings. Horses clacked slowly along the cobblestones all around them.

"Of course I am," said Victor irritably. "But I have so much work to do . . ."

The months went by, and Victor stopped attending lectures almost entirely. Neither of his two professors objected to his absences, even though he declined to tell them the nature of the research he was engaged in. What had started off as a sort of brandy-induced dream had become an obsession. He had found himself more spacious lodgings – the upper two floors of one of Ingolstadt's large town houses – and in the attic there he had constructed an extensive laboratory. In the very middle of the room stood a glass-sided tank.

Working over twenty hours each day, remembering only once or twice a week that he should eat, and sleeping on a filthy mat on the laboratory floor, he spent as much of his time as possible working out complicated chemical equations and experimenting with them at the crude bench he had built along one of the attic's sloping walls. He had started out by believing that through the mighty power of electricity he could bring a corpse back to life and, perhaps, give it a mind: now he was determined to do better than that – to create a thinking human being from scratch.

No! This creature would be better than any human being. Victor had grown to have a sour view of those around him. On the few occasions when he left the house, they laughed at his ragged clothes, his spindly frame and his unkempt hair. They – the rest of humanity – were lesser beings than he was because they were incapable of recognizing his genius. The creature he would bring into existence would be even better than he was. It would be untainted by the pettiness, the narrow-mindedness, of the world.

Very infrequently he saw the faces of people he knew he had once loved – whom he still did love, whenever he had the time. William and his father and his dead mother and Henry Clerval and, more than any of them, Elizabeth. Even less often did it occur to him that the power of his urge to create the next race of humankind might be driving him into insanity.

He had had the idea that every single part of the human body contained the seed of every other part: that from a toe or even a fingernail all of the rest could be grown – the face, the eyes, the stomach, the bones, the heart and even the brain. Where the idea had come from he did not know: perhaps Professor Krempe had made some remark that had set Victor off along this train of thought, but it was more likely that he'd come across it in one of those much-read books on alchemy that he'd brought from Geneva and which he'd dutifully, on Professor Krempe's instructions, burned.

But if he were to grow a body, perhaps from some of his own flesh, he needed to find the chemicals that would nurture the growth. He followed one sequence of theory and experiment after another until, in late October of that year, inspiration blossomed in his fevered mind. For forty-three hours nonstop he sat at his desk, scribbling so intensely that often his pencil tore through the paper. He ate nothing – hunger was a trivial sensation in comparison with the excitement he felt when he saw each of his chemical equations unfold into the next, developing his initial idea into something vastly more complex yet which contained a simple beauty of its own.

"Yes!" he shouted. At last the correct formula lay on the page in front of him. The diagram of what he needed looked so obvious, and the chemicals required to create the compound so easily available, that he was surprised it had never occurred to anyone before.

"Yes!" he yelled again. "Yes! I have it!"

It was three o'clock in the morning. The

tenants on the lower floors started shouting, telling the mad scientist above them to keep quiet. Victor Frankenstein collapsed onto his mattress with a knowing smile on his face. He slept more than twice around the clock.

The tank that Victor had built in the middle of his laboratory was taller than a man and required a huge volume of chemicals and nutrients to fill it. Money was no problem for him – his father had established a more than ample allowance for him at one of Ingolstadt's many banks – but the sheer physical problem of getting the liquid chemicals up to his attic laboratory was more difficult to solve. In the end, he employed odd-job men to go to different apothecary shops and return with five-gallon jars of the various substances he needed.

He drew the powders and nutrients required to complete the mixture from the university's stocks. He explained to an inquisitive Professor Krempe that he needed them in order to prove that Paracelsus had lied when he'd claimed that a particular formulation had enabled him to create silver. The professor seemed to relish this explanation and inquired no further. It was a full week before everything was ready. Now all Victor had to do was wait for the next thunderstorm.

Then, one evening, it happened. He stood in the doorway and gazed around his laboratory. There were jars everywhere, each bearing a label in his spidery handwriting. He'd left a narrow path among them from the door to the great tank in the middle of the room. Outside, the night sky was riven yet again by a dart of lightning. The large roof windows of the attic shook in their frames as the gale beat at them. He took a deep breath and raised his lamp higher. This was going to be very dangerous.

First he needed light. Picking his way around and over the jars, he lit the various lamps that hung on the walls and finally a cluster of candles on his bench.

Then he went into a frenzy of movement. It was important that the chemicals be added to the tank in the correct order. Each of the jars was very heavy – and seemed much heavier because of his poor state of health. By the time the tank was full he was staggering and clutching at his aching chest as he took painful gasps, struggling to breathe. He allowed himself to rest for half an hour, listening to the thunder roar and thump in the heavens above and praying that it would continue long enough for him to finish his experiment. At last, pulling himself together with a conscious effort, he forced himself to his feet. Although the most dangerous part of the experiment would come later, next was the part he was least looking forward to.

Shrugging, he picked up a scalpel from his bench. The flickering light of the lamps made the steel blade seem almost as if it were malevolently alive. To test its sharpness he drew the edge hesitantly across his thumb; he felt no pain, but a line of blood droplets appeared immediately.

It was certainly sharp enough for what he had to do. In a way, he wished that it wasn't. He gashed the left leg of his trousers with the scalpel and pulled the cloth apart. Through the rip he could see his thigh.

"The side of the thigh has fewer pain sensors than any other part of the body," he said out loud, trying to reassure himself. "You'll hardly feel a thing,"

The words were only a slight comfort, because a voice inside him was saying, "Yes, but the thigh still has some pain sensors."

If he waited any longer he'd be unable to go through with this. Gulping, he closed his eyes and plunged the scalpel into the flesh of his thigh and, before he could think any more about it, gouged away a strip of flesh.

The pain was excruciating. He thought he was going to throw up or faint, or both, but somehow he managed to keep control of himself. Opening his eyes again, he grabbed some clean cotton from the bench and crammed it into the wound.

Another thunderbolt crashed across the heavens, and at last he was able to allow himself a scream of agony. As the echoes of his scream died away, he leaned forward in his chair, watching pain-induced shapes floating in front of his eyes. When at last his vision cleared he saw the scalpel lying in the dust of the laboratory floor and the strip of bleeding flesh in his left hand.

He put the flesh – his own flesh – carefully on a clean dish on the bench and seized a roll of gauze. It took him only a minute to bind up his wound and then, at first clutching the edge of the bench for support, he was able to stand. Swaying, he released the bench. He should have added a strong dose of morphine to the list of requisitions, he thought ruefully. But there was no time to waste. The thunderstorm could end at any moment.

Hobbling, kicking aside empty jars with his left leg, he hurled the strip of flesh into the chemicals in the tank and then threw open one of the attic's huge skylights. At once he was battered in the face by the ferocious, wind-whipped rain. He put up an arm to shield himself and stumbled back to the bench. Underneath it was a kite he had made while waiting for all the chemicals to arrive.

The kite had two cords. One was of ordinary string, and this was the reel that he would hold. The other was metal. He attached it to a heavy lump of steel which he then dropped into the tank where the piece of his thigh floated gorily, tendrils of blood forming on the surface before slowly sinking.

He was going to pass out from the pain unless he hurried. "That's it!" he thought to himself. "Concentrate on the pain. It'll take your mind off the recklessness of what you're just about to do."

Somehow he got himself back up to the skylight. The wind and the rain lashed at him so hard that he had to close his eyes. He lifted the kite out into the gale, and almost at once it was snatched from his hand. When he dared to open his eyes again, he could see the kite swooping briefly over the roof of the building opposite, and then climbing up to the heavy, lightning-lit thunder-clouds. The reel in his hands thrummed as if it were a wild beast seeking freedom. Behind him he could hear the wire rattling angrily against the side of the tank. For a minute, maybe two, the storm seemed to abate, causing Victor to cry out once more, this time in frustration. Then a colossal crash of thunder shook the entire building.

Victor Frankenstein shut his eyes again, expecting to die. The metal cord brushed his sleeve. If the powerful electricity of the lightning . . .

But no. The tossing of the kite, far above in the sky, tugged the wire away from him just in time to prevent him from being electrocuted. And then the lightning struck. The entire sky was illuminated. Even through his closed eyelids Victor was almost dazzled by the glare.

He felt a sudden heat near him, and then heard the chemicals in the tank churning furiously.

It had worked!

Groggily opening his eyes, he saw a charred line running across the floor of the laboratory. The bolt of electricity had melted the wire as it had passed through it, and the hot gobbets of metal had fallen down onto the wooden boards. Nevertheless, he realized as the chemicals in the tank still churned, enough electricity had survived. Enough to initiate the generation of life.

Unless his calculations had been wrong.

Forcing himself not to think about that, he let his numb fingers drop the reel of string. He took a few clumsy steps in the direction of the tank, and fell headlong among the empty jars. He felt the pain of a hundred jagged edges of glass biting into his body, but then darkness filled him.

FEVER

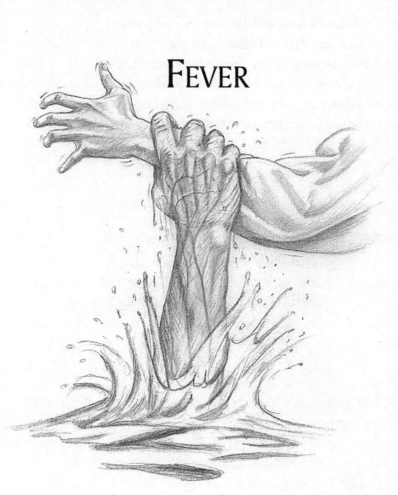

He came to his senses an unknown time later to find himself in a brightly lit, clean-smelling room. Someone was wiping his forehead with a damp cloth. For a few minutes Victor simply enjoyed the sensation, not even thinking about where he might be, but then the memories flooded back. He moaned.

"Take it easy, old chap," said a voice.

"Wh– Where am I?"

"You're in my lodgings."

Now Victor recognized the voice.

"Henry!" he said. "But how did I . . . ?"

"I found you," said Henry. "I hadn't seen you for weeks, and was worried about you, so the day after the great storm I skipped my lectures and came across to your place. You were lying in a mass of blood and broken glass and rainwater. I . . . ." Henry paused momentarily, clearly still upset from the experience – "I thought you were dead."

Victor reached up a hand to his face. He could feel the scabs that had formed there. As if this were a signal, all the other parts of his body then began to register pain, complaining about the lacerations they had received. The deep wound in his thigh was a more ponderous ache.

"What else did you see?" he said wearily, turning over onto his side.

"Equipment. Jars. Some big thing in the middle of the room." Henry had recovered himself, and he spoke cheerfully. "I wasn't really looking, dear chap. I was more concerned about you than about your scientific paraphernalia."

"How long have I been here?" said Victor desperately.

"Only three days."

Three days? Only three days? Three days that he should have spent watching his creation grow. What might have happened to it by now?

"I must get back there!" Victor cried.

"No, you mustn't, Victor." Now Henry's voice was firm, almost strict. "What you must do is stay here a few more days until your fever lets up. You're not fit to go out. You're not fit even to climb out of bed. Now be quiet. I'm going to try you with some thin soup and see if you can keep it down."

A little later Victor felt a warm spoon against his lips and instinctively opened his mouth to let a little of the soup dribble in.

"But I must go back there," he protested weakly. "My experiment –"

"– is safely under lock and key," said Henry. "It can wait a week or so until you're well enough to continue with it."

"You don't understand," began Victor, and then realized he couldn't tell even his best friend about the experiment. Henry was not profoundly religious, but even he would be appalled by what Victor was trying to do. He would keep silent about it, of course, but if anyone else should ever learn . . . And if the Church authorities should somehow hear that Victor had been attempting to create life – to usurp the role of God – he would surely be arrested and perhaps hanged.

"All I understand," said Henry, "is that you have a fever and need to rest – and that's the end of it."

Under Henry's care, Victor slowly regained his health, but it was another ten days before he was well enough to make his way back across Ingolstadt to his own lodgings. He could see that he hurt his old friend's feelings when he refused to allow Henry to accompany him, but there was no way that he could risk Henry seeing whatever the tank might now contain. In the end he mumbled something meaningless, embraced Henry while showering him with thanks, and climbed aboard the hired carriage alone.

When he reached his lodgings and paid the coachman, he paused in the street for a moment and looked up at the front of the building. From here there was no sign that anything at all unusual had taken place thirteen nights ago. He clenched his fists. What might be waiting for him in the laboratory? He had to find out. Sucking in air through pursed lips, he pushed open the door of the building and began to climb the stairs, feeling in his pocket for the key.

At the door of his laboratory, he forced himself to calm down, taking several deep, measured breaths before putting the key in the lock. With any luck, his experiment had been a failure. Otherwise . . .

The door swung open with a creak. Sunlight shafted in through the roof windows to reveal a scene of absolute devastation. Shards of glass lay scattered all over the floor, as if a bomb had been detonated. There was a rank smell in the air.

He took a nervous step into the laboratory, and stared at the tank. Its contents were the murky brown of dried blood. Treading cautiously, glass crunching beneath his boots, he made his way to the tank and

peeped over the rim. There was only the smooth, undisturbed surface of the liquid. He didn't know whether to laugh out loud with relief or to cry with disappointment. Confused thoughts and troubled emotions ran through his mind. He had failed, it was true, but maybe that was for the best. He sighed and relaxed slightly. Then, from the liquid, a huge hand shot out to grab him.

Henry Clerval watched the back of the carriage Victor had hired retreating down the busy Ingolstadt street, and frowned. Victor had fought against his confinement all the time he had been staying with Henry, and was obviously still in a state of high turmoil and anxiety when he left. It was true that his physical fever had cleared up entirely – although the scabs on his face and body had not completely disappeared – but that was obviously only half the story. Now that he was gone, Henry began to fret that his friend might still be suffering from some kind of mental fever.

He should have insisted on accompanying Victor back to his lodgings. He didn't care what the experiment was that Victor had been so obsessively secretive about. It was probably important to other scientists, who might steal the idea, but it was certainly of no concern to Henry, who didn't know the first thing about science.

"I should have gone with him," Henry thought again. "I should have clung to him like a limpet, and made him take me with him."

He put his hand in his pocket, looking for coins. He found a little small change, but certainly not enough to hire another carriage and go after Victor. He waited a few seconds longer in the street trying to decide what to do. Then, his mind made up, he dashed inside to lock up his room. It would take him the best part of half an hour to walk to his friend's lodgings, but he knew that the only way to quell his fears was to see Victor safely confined once more. Minutes later he was dodging the traffic of the Ingolstadt streets as he trudged determinedly toward the far side of the town.

The creature that Victor had grown from the shred of his own thigh sat up in its bath of chemicals and nutrients. Its hand still gripped his arm. Victor tried to pull himself away. The thing's body looked as if it had been flayed. Its eyes were closed. He had never seen a face so hideous. And the creature was huge – upright, it would be half as tall again as any normal man.

The being refused to release his arm, however much Victor wriggled and squirmed. Yes, it was of human form – more or less. Perhaps it would have been less horrific had it not been a cruel mimicry of the human shape: then it could have been merely an unknown creature of gargantuan size. But, because it had vague traces of humanity about it, it chilled his heart.

"Let – go – of – me," Victor grunted, with each word trying to haul himself out of the monster's clutch. "Let – go." He knew the command was useless even as he spoke. How could the creature understand words? Still he tried to yank himself away, shouting at the thing.

The creature's blank face bore no malevolence, and yet it revolted him. This was an abomination! In trying to play the game of God he had been guilty of committing a crime against all humanity – that same humanity which he had been hoping to aid!

He had created a grossly terrifying caricature of a human being. What if its mind were as hideously disfigured as that repellent face . . . if, in fact, the thing had a mind . . .

He reached behind him, searching for a scalpel – if need be he would hack this creature's vast hand off at the wrist – but his bench was out of reach. Stooping, he snatched up a piece of broken glass and with all his might plunged its sharp edge into the creature's forearm. The monster let out a howl of distress and released its grip just long enough for Victor to stagger back, coughing and spluttering, until he crashed against the back wall of the laboratory. He couldn't take his eyes off the creature, even though he desperately wanted to.

Its flesh was changing now that it was exposed to the air. The flayed appearance faded as traceries of leathery-looking skin formed across the surface, and then joined up, the pieces gradually forming a tough, almost shiny hide. Even as Victor watched, the gash he had inflicted on the monster's forearm knitted itself together and slowly vanished under an advancing layer of skin that looked like parchment. The creature roared again, and clamped its two huge hands on the edge of the tank.

Spreadeagled against the laboratory wall, Victor watched as his creation, moving with apparent difficulty, hauled itself upright. It was having to learn everything for the first time, Victor realized. Waves of dirty brown liquid washed out of the tank to splatter on the floor. As the colossal parody of the human form rose to its feet, the transformation of its skin proceeded ever more quickly.

"Oh, God," Victor said out loud. "I wish I'd never left Geneva."

Had he only been able to shake off Henry Clerval a few days ago the creature might have been man-sized but, lying here in the tank, it had continued to grow until he had disturbed it. If he had been delayed another few days . . . He shuddered at the thought.

Victor had no weapons in the laboratory, apart from his set of scalpels – and these would be useless against something as enormous and monstrous as the creature had become. Part of him, the part that was a scientist, recognized that his emotions were just a throwback – if someone is sufficiently different from the rest of the tribe he must die – but the inner voice of the scientist was drowned out by the tide of sheer revulsion that swept through him.

Yet again the monster roared wordlessly. The windows shook. Its eyes opened, and turned to stare at him. They were a hideous, dirty yellow.

"If I could only kill it, no one need know," thought Victor. Then he heard footsteps on the stairs far below. He ran for the door.

"Well met, Henry," said Victor, almost bumping into his friend.

"What's going on, Victor?" Henry grasped the banister. "You look dreadful. Has your fever returned?"

"No." Victor drew the back of his sleeve across his sweating forehead. "But" – he sought desperately for some kind of excuse as he took Henry firmly by the elbow and turned him around – "but the shock of seeing my laboratory again may have been a little too much for me. The damage! You told me of the devastation, but I didn't believe you – not really. I don't want to look at it again – not for a while – not at the destruction of everything I've been working on these past months. It's too much to bear, my friend."

"Victor," said Henry, barely able to conceal the frustration in his voice as he was hurried down the stairs. "Victor, just what is it that you've been doing up there?"

"It would be impossible to explain to someone not trained in the sciences," said Victor, trying to control his breathlessness. "It was an experiment. It failed. There's nothing more you need to know."

He had to get out of here. He had to leave Ingolstadt. If anyone connected him with the monstrosity he had created he would surely be put to death. Let the authorities deal with the . . . the thing. Weren't they paid to cope with emergencies?

He had no clear thought in his head but flight.

"But –"

"There aren't any 'buts', Henry. I just want to leave this terrible place behind me for a few days. If you can miss your lectures, let's find ourselves an inn in the country somewhere, far from Ingolstadt, where I can recuperate from the shock I've just had and at the same time repay you for your goodness in nursing me through my fever. I can buy some new clothes for us both as we go."

They were at the front door. Suddenly there was a huge bellow from the top of the house.

"What on earth was that?" exclaimed Henry, shaking off Victor's hand.

"A dog. Just a dog. It's not important. Let's get out

of here. I need to get to the countryside. Will you come with me, old friend?"

Victor reached out for Henry's arms and was only just able to stop himself from shaking the man. "Will you?"

Henry squinted at him suspiciously, and then his face cleared.

"Of course, old man. Anything you say. It's about time I took a break from my studies."

"And will you promise me you'll say nothing about anything you've seen and heard here?"

Henry forced a laugh. "You scientists," he said. "You think that I would understand anything about what I've seen?"

"Then let's go. Now. Let's go. Please, Henry. If I delay any longer I'll . . ."

Henry shrugged.

"Let's go," he echoed.

DEATH IN GENEVA

They spent two weeks away from Ingolstadt, wandering through the foothills of the Bavarian Alps, and spending their nights in the first welcoming inn they came across each evening. Although the end of the year was approaching fast, the weather was surprisingly mild. Only on one day did the snow fall heavily, and then they remained in their inn, surrounded by countryfolk who, like themselves, believed that the best way to endure a blizzard was by sipping a tankard of beer beside a warm log fire.

Sometimes Henry pressed Victor to talk about the nature of his experiments, but Victor refused to tell him anything. After being glowered at often enough, Henry stopped asking. Victor himself was trying to forget what he had done – and what might be happening as a result, even at that moment, in Ingolstadt. He imagined a different past for himself, a past in which he had never left Geneva. Perhaps he and Elizabeth might have been married by now.

At last Henry insisted that he must return to the university and his studies of ancient languages. He had abandoned the classics some while before in order to concentrate on ancient Persian and Sanskrit, and he was eager to pick up where he had left off. After tending Victor through his fever and then taking this trip, he had missed nearly a month of lectures. If he didn't return soon he feared his professor would refuse to have him back.

"That's the difference between the sciences and the arts, Victor," he explained. "Professor Krempe will assume you have been busy with research. My Professor Mannheim will assume I've been idling – which is exactly what I have been doing. We must go back. I must."

Sadly, Victor agreed. At every inn they'd visited, he had kept his ears open for any reports of a monster in the town of Ingolstadt, but had heard nothing. He turned away so Henry wouldn't see the wave of revulsion that passed across his face. Perhaps the hideous being he had created hadn't escaped from the laboratory but had died, unlamented, in the tank in which it had been grown. He wasn't sure what to think, but felt certain he would have heard something if the monster was on the loose in the town. They hired horses from a staging post and headed back to Ingolstadt, arriving the next day.

There were several letters waiting for Victor at his lodgings. Tucking them under his arm, he trudged up the stairs, remembering the last time he had climbed them and the horror he had discovered at the top.

But this time he didn't hesitate. The time away with Henry had improved his spirits immensely. He felt as if nothing could dishearten him now – not even the discovery of a vast dead body that he would have to dispose of somehow. Brimming with confidence, he climbed the last flight. What he saw at the top made his confidence drain away.

The door to his rooms had been flattened out on the landing, blasted from its frame by a mighty blow from inside. Splinters of wood dangled around the opening. The monster had not died. Victor had been deluding himself during these past two weeks. Surely such a vile creature could not survive for more than an hour, he had told himself every night. And surely he would have heard if it had escaped. But it had escaped – unless it was still here, waiting for him.

Victor tiptoed into the room, stepping on the door. The wood groaned under his weight and he flinched, putting his arms up as if he expected to be attacked. Controlling his fear, he took another pace. As soon as he was inside he relaxed. All his senses told him that he was alone. Wherever the creature might have gone, it was not here. He looked through the dusky light at the wooden stairway that led up to the laboratory, and plucked up a little more courage. He had to see. He had to know.

He found the laboratory much as he'd left it. There was still the litter of broken glass: tomorrow he would

have to start sweeping it away. There was a smell of blood in the air, and he realized almost immediately that it came from the tank. He crept forward and peered through the glass. The tank contained only liquid. The monster had gone – or perhaps it had dissolved back into the chemicals. Victor let out a deep breath. It seemed to him that he was free.

Much later that night he discovered that most of his bedding was gone. For a moment, slightly fuddled by the brandy that he had drunk with his supper, he thought that he had been robbed, but then he realized what must have really happened. The ghastly monster he had created had seized the bedding to wrap around itself. Victor sobered up instantly. Wherever the monster had gone, he was sure it was no longer in Ingolstadt – he would certainly have been told about it in the grocery shop where he had bought the food for his dinner. He imagined the creature roaming through the forests that surrounded the town on three sides, catching small creatures for its own meal. He remembered its horrible roar, and wondered if other people – forest folk – were now hearing it under the pale moonlight.

He shook his head. The monster had taken itself out of his life, and that was good enough for him. Tomorrow he would get rid of everything in his laboratory and start the long, slow process of forgetting all about his insane, foolhardy experiment. Tomorrow, too, he would have to face up to Professor Krempe, who would undoubtedly want to know what the brightest of his students had been doing these past few months with nothing to show for it. But that was tomorrow. Tonight was tonight, and Victor was exhausted. Not bothering to remove his clothes, he threw himself down on the bare mattress, dragged a pillow under his head, and within moments was asleep.

It was only the next morning that he remembered the bundle of letters he had brought up from the front hall. The first two were from Professor Krempe, demanding to know where Victor was. Didn't he realize that it was one of the duties of any student at Ingolstadt University to attend at least some lectures? Victor threw them aside. He could answer them well enough later in the day, when he confronted the professor in his lair.

The next one was addressed in handwriting he knew well: Elizabeth's. He tore the letter open eagerly, and imagined he could smell her scent rising from the single sheet of paper. He ran his eyes down the first side, turned the paper over, read the second side, and then started again from the beginning. He glanced at the date at the top, and realized that she had written to him nearly seven weeks before.

Dearest Victor,

It seems such a long time since I have seen your smile or heard your voice. Your studies at the university must be arduous indeed!

Darling William is growing to look very much like his elder brother! And like his elder brother he has developed a passion for "matters scientific" as he likes to describe them at the dinner table while telling us about the frogs, leeches and who knows what else that he keeps in tanks in his room. As he grows up, he and Justine are becoming more like brother and sister than ever.

Your father is unchanged but . . . growing older. I know he would like to see his much beloved son again soon.

Justine is in love! A nice boy from the village, who goes by the name of Werner, is the object of her affections. We have all become very fond of him, though William is terribly unsympathetic whenever Justine goes all moon-eyed about her young man.

Your father, of course, assumes that the lovebirds will marry soon, and he would prefer it to be tomorrow so that he could give them a great wedding party all the sooner. He has confided in me that he has treated Justine in his will as if she were his daughter. He also proposes to hire young Werner as an extra gardener, and to give the newly-weds the gatehouse as their wedding present. And all this time Justine has still not made up her mind for certain!

Oh, Victor, all this talk of marriage makes me long for the moment when once again I can look into your eyes and know that . . .

The second page expressed her love for him at very great and at times almost embarrassing length. She had written very little about herself. Over and over again she told him how much she wanted to see him.

"And you soon will!" said Victor to the air. "Even if I can only return for a few days, I'll be there soon."

He held the letter crumpled to his chest, and once again believed he could smell her scent. Elizabeth was so lovely – so very different from the thing he had created in his arrogance. The thought of her walking by his side across the even lawns of Castle Frankenstein, her laughter tinkling in his ears . . . He sat on the edge of his bed, his eyes tightly shut, for a long time, thinking about her. Once or twice during his years in Ingolstadt he'd seen a pretty face in the street and been momentarily distracted, but Elizabeth had never been far from his heart.

Dizzily he reached for the next letter. Again he recognized the handwriting: this time it was his father's. Without much interest he broke open the seal and several sheets of paper fell to the floor. Gathering them up, putting them in order, Victor noticed that this letter had been written some three weeks after Elizabeth's. Feeling as if he were doing a duty, he started to read. A few moments later he was standing upright, horrified by what his father had to say. His beloved William was dead!

Victor read the paragraph again, refusing to believe it. His little brother, whom he had last seen sobbing into Justine's dress, had been murdered – strangled! Worse still – if anything could be worse – Justine had been arrested and thrown into prison on the suspicion that she had committed the crime.

"She could no more have killed William than I could have myself!" shouted Victor, though there was no one to hear.

Forgetting all about the ruined laboratory in the attic, Victor quickly began packing his clothes. If he could find a good coachman who was willing to take him, he could be at home in Geneva within the week.

"Henry!" he said out loud. "I must see Henry." Henry had been desperate to resume his studies, but Victor must tell him about all this before leaving Ingolstadt. It was likely his old friend would want to return to Geneva with him – he had treated William as if he were a somewhat exasperating but much-loved younger brother, and Elizabeth and Justine as if they were his own sisters. However much Victor wanted to leave Ingolstadt right now, this instant, he must see Henry before he went.

Tears ran down Victor's face. The law could sometimes be shockingly swift in Geneva – for all he knew Justine might have been hanged already. Even so, he had to get home as soon as possible – if for no other reason than to console Elizabeth and his father. But he hoped beyond all hope that he would be there in time to speak at the trial, to explain to the magistrates the impossibility that Justine could have in any way harmed the child who had been in her care for so long. Justine – the woman had been incapable of swatting a fly. Surely they would listen to him! Surely they would believe him! Henry would speak out for her as well.

When Victor had finished packing – everything that he wanted to take away from Ingolstadt squeezed into a big suitcase – he went down to the street and waited impatiently for a carriage. At last one came. Victor blurted out the address of Henry's lodgings. "And," he added, "would you be willing to carry both of us all the way to Geneva?"

"That'll depend on the price," said the coachman as the vehicle lurched into motion.

"I'll pay you handsomely," said Victor. "More than you would think of asking. Much, much more."

"You're the sort of customer I like," said the coachman with a cackle, cracking his whip above the heads of the horses. "I can get you there in a week."

The man was as good as his word. As soon as Henry slammed the door of the carriage – just as Victor had suspected, his old friend insisted on returning to Geneva with him – the coachman began to push the horses to the limit of their endurance. They reached

Geneva in seven days, as the coachman had promised.

All through the journey, the suspicion grew in Victor's mind that he knew the murderer. He remembered the malevolent stare the monster had directed at him. Could the beast somehow have discovered where the Frankensteins lived? It seemed impossible, but . . .

What was worse was that, if the creature was so inspired by evil that it could kill an innocent youth, how many other members of Victor's family might it murder before its thirst for vengeance was satisfied? But no: this line of thought was taking him too far. There was no evidence at all that the monster was even alive, let alone capable of malevolent acts. And it was an even more ridiculous idea to think that it could have tracked down Victor's family in Geneva. This was all wild speculation. Then he remembered that night when, on the way home from Professor Krempe's, he'd engaged in some other wild speculation. His instincts had guided him then. Perhaps they were guiding him now . . .

Victor churned these thoughts over and over in his mind all the way to Geneva. Henry found him very poor company.

The trial of Justine Moritz began the morning after Victor and Henry arrived. It was held in the Central Court of Justice in Geneva before a group of three magistrates. Victor settled himself uneasily on one of the hard benches. Elizabeth was on one side of him, his father on the other. Henry had decided to sit on the far side of the timbered room so that, if he were called to give evidence about Justine's character, he would not seem too closely connected with the Frankenstein family. Victor breathed deeply. The courtroom smelled of old fear.

Half an hour passed before the three magistrates, dressed in long red and black robes, made their entrance. All the people in the courtroom got to their feet and waited as the magistrates seated themselves behind the imposing oak table that more or less filled the platform at the end of the room. Then a pair of burly prison officers brought in Justine.

Victor stared. In the years since he had left Geneva, Justine had grown from a very pretty girl into a beautiful woman, but there was still an innocence in her face which made it impossible for anyone to believe that she could have committed such a savage murder. Surely she would be declared guiltless at once. He turned to look at Elizabeth. Her blue eyes were filled with tears.

"I'm sure she'll be freed," he whispered reassuringly. "Just look at her."

"No," Elizabeth whispered back, "they'll hang her, whether she's shown to be innocent or not. She's too beautiful for them. They'll hang her to show the rest of the world that their decisions aren't affected by a pretty face – that their justice is fair to everyone."

Victor turned back to look at the court. Before the magistrates had appeared the people had been gossiping and joking; now they were deadly silent as the clerk of the court read out the accusation against Justine. Victor found it impossible to concentrate on what the man was saying. Too many ideas, too many guilts and worries, were chasing each other around inside his head.

". . . that on this past day of . . . you did deliberately and cruelly . . . the boy entrusted to your care . . ."

As soon as the clerk had finished speaking, the prosecutor leapt to his feet. Victor was horrified as he listened. Until now he had not known how convincing the evidence against Justine was – or could be made to appear.

William had disappeared during an afternoon picnic in which the whole family – except Justine, who had been visiting her aunt – had participated. That night Justine had gone missing; the following morning she had been discovered wandering aimlessly near the spot where William's corpse had been found. On being shown his body she had fallen into a faint, and had had to be confined to her bed for some days.

Meanwhile, a servant had found a locket in one of Justine's pockets and recognized it as the memento which William always wore under his shirt. It had belonged to his dead mother. From the lips of the prosecutor the evidence sounded very convincing, and Victor's eyes kept slipping from the man's eagerly accusatory face to Justine's, and back again. The prosecutor described the bruises on William's neck.

"Clearly no normal woman would have had the strength to inflict such damage," he said, spittle flying from his mouth. "This must have been the work of a madwoman." He pointed dramatically at Justine.

"That madwoman!" he shouted.

As he sat down, pandemonium erupted in the courtroom. Some people in the crowd were yelling that Justine was innocent, but the majority were demanding just as loudly that she be taken from the courtroom and hanged immediately. Victor had cringed when the prosecutor described the strength of the hands that had strangled his brother. He knew of only one pair of hands that had that strength. All of the gloomy suspicions he had during the journey to Geneva came back to him. Somehow the creature had made its way here . . .

He woke from his miserable thoughts to realise that Justine was speaking. Yes, she admitted, she had been out of the house for the whole night after William's disappearance, but this was because she was looking for him. Coming home after an evening with her aunt, she had learned of the boy's disappearance from a man she had met and had immediately set out to try to find him. She had slept briefly in a barn during the early hours of the morning, then continued her search. By the time she was found at dawn she was at her wits' end through exhaustion and anxiety. She had no idea how the locket had come to be in her pocket.

Her tale sounded appallingly weak to Victor, but Elizabeth took his hand and whispered to him: "That's obviously what happened! Surely they'll realize that."

"I thought you said they'd hang her anyway," he muttered grimly.

"Yes, but —" Elizabeth fell silent as a clerk of the court gestured to her to come to the witness stand.

There was little by way of hard evidence that Elizabeth could offer, but she was able to describe how much Justine and William had loved each other, and how much the family had come to regard Justine as being almost of their own blood. She declared to the magistrates that William had been like a brother to her: if she were firmly convinced of Justine's innocence, should not they, who had never known her or the boy, be even more so? Elizabeth's testimony was followed by Baron Frankenstein's. He repeated much of what she had said.

Victor was in an agony of guilt, but he didn't know what to do. If he told the court about his belief that his little brother had been killed by a monster which he, Victor, had created in an Ingolstadt attic, they would laugh at his feverish imagination — and become even more determined to hang Justine. If they would only believe him, of course, they would hang him in her place, but they wouldn't believe him: they would simply think he was raving or lying. A few more witnesses were called and then the trial was declared over. The verdict, the clerk informed the court, would be handed down tomorrow. Everyone stood up as the magistrates solemnly filed out and Justine was led away to her cell in the basement beneath the courthouse.

Elizabeth tugged at Victor's arm. "Come on," she said. "We've done as much as we can. It's time for us to go home and pray that God will touch the magistrates' hearts tonight." Victor continued to stare straight ahead, his mind in a ferment. "Perhaps they would have believed me," he thought. If only I'd . . ."

"Yes, dear lad, come on," said Baron Frankenstein, pulling at Victor's other arm. "Elizabeth and I need your support." The old man was choking with emotion. Victor let them lead him out of the courtroom and into their carriage. His eyes blank, he saw nothing of the countryside as they drove rapidly back to Castle Frankenstein.

The next morning, Justine Moritz was declared guilty, and publicly hanged.

ON MONTANVERT

The next two weeks were a miserable time for everyone at Castle Frankenstein. After the trial, Henry returned to Ingolstadt and Victor spent much of every day alone in his room with the curtains drawn. His earlier suspicions had hardened into certainties. He had created a living being in the hope of improving the lot of humanity: the result was that two of the people dearest to him in the world were dead. If he had murdered them himself his emotions would have been easier to tackle. As it was, he knew that they were dead not through any malice but through his own folly. Their blood was on his hands – he was honest enough with himself to admit this – yet he had not intended for them to die. He was guilty of murder, but he was not a murderer.

One night, unable to sleep, he was staring out through his bedroom window at the moonlit lawn. From the shrubbery there emerged what he thought at first was a trick of the shadows. Then he saw that it was some great beast. It was too far away for him to be able to see it clearly, but he imagined that it turned its head to look up at his window – to look directly at him. Then, in the blinking of an eye, it was moving at impossible speed across the silver grass until it was lost from his sight.

"No normal woman would have had the strength to inflict such damage," the prosecutor had said. And neither, Victor told himself, would any normal man.

It was Elizabeth who finally roused him from his orgy of self-recrimination. One day she knocked at his bedroom door and then, hearing no reply, beat on it with her fist. Finally, ignoring all decorum, she simply threw the door open and stormed in.

"Don't be such a self-pitying fool, Victor!" she shouted, dragging the curtains open so that sunlight flooded into the room. "Get up out of bed now!"

"But I'm not wearing –"

"I spend every Friday nursing the poor at the cottage hospital so there's no need to be coy," she snapped angrily. "Here" – she picked up a bundle of his clothes from the chair and hurled them at him – "get yourself dressed and come downstairs. Your father has lost one son to a murderer. At the moment he feels he's lost another to the same murderer. He's pining away – dying visibly – because you're being so completely selfish, Victor. I'll look out of the window while you put your clothes on, but I'm not leaving this room until you leave it with me."

With a last furious flash from her bright blue eyes she turned away. "It stinks in here," she said in an exasperated voice as she struggled to open the window. Numb with embarrassment, Victor pulled himself into the first garments that came to hand.

"One of the peacocks is spreading his tail," said Elizabeth more gently from the window. "If you've finished dressing you could come and look." He joined her, aware that his chin was unshaven and that his shirt-tail was hanging out.

"Where?" he said.

She pointed. The feathers were glorious. Then the bird let out a raucous honk and for the first time in weeks Victor felt himself beginning to smile.

"A very pretty sight, but not such a pretty sound," he said softly.

"I imagine you think the same of me, right now," said Elizabeth.

"No. You were right to say those things."

He put his hand on her shoulder and turned her to face him. "I have been selfish, but there's more to the deaths of William and Justine than I can tell even you." She gazed back at him.

"Victor –" she began, then stopped, moving a half-pace away from him.

"You are the brightest part of my life, Elizabeth. I would like . . . I would like . . ."

She skipped away from him and started picking up discarded garments from the floor. "To marry me? Oh, of course we'll marry each other – I decided that long before you went away to Ingolstadt."

Victor laughed out loud. "Elizabeth!" he cried.

Dropping the clothes, she came into his embrace.

The baron was delighted when they told him they were going to get married, and hugged each of them again and again. He ordered two cases of his best wine from the cellars, and over the next few weeks drank most of it himself. It was obvious to both Victor and

Elizabeth that he had been hoping for years that they would eventually marry, but had held himself back from saying so.

Only at night, lying awake as the wind howled, did Victor think about the two deaths he believed he had caused . . .

The baron declared the wedding should take place in three months' time – any earlier would be to insult the memories of William and Justine. Victor and Elizabeth wanted to marry as soon as possible, but they recognized the force of the old man's argument. Moreover, Victor needed some time to himself. It seemed paradoxical that he loved to be near Elizabeth, yet also craved solitude. He had to confront the emotions that still battled within him, and he couldn't do this when she was there. He remembered fondly the trip to the Alps he had enjoyed with Henry and how relaxing it had been.

"I have to go away for a while," he said one morning at breakfast.

Elizabeth looked offended. Victor reached out across the linen tablecloth and touched the ends of her fingers with his. "There are things that happened at Ingolstadt that I must work to forget," he said earnestly. Elizabeth snatched away her hand.

"I see," she said icily.

Victor hesitated. "No, I don't mean there was another woman, Elizabeth. It's just that I was doing an experiment, and – and it went wrong. The repercussions of my failure may have caused great grief to others. Even though I didn't intend that to happen,

I still feel guilty about it all. I need to spend a little while by myself, walking in the mountains, thinking things through. I'll be a better husband to you, Elizabeth, if I do."

At the other end of the table the baron snorted. "Never bothered with such stuff in my day," he muttered. But neither Victor nor Elizabeth were listening to him.

"If it's important," she said.

"It is."

"Then go with my blessing."

In the valley of Chamonix, high in the Alps, the air was pure and good. Victor breathed it appreciatively as he crested a small ridge and saw a carpet of spring flowers stretching away to a little river far below. He dropped onto the grass and propped his stick beside him. In his knapsack he had some bread and cheese that he'd bought at the inn where he'd stayed the previous night. He dug them out, inspected them critically, then began to eat hungrily, washing down the food with swigs of beer.

Before leaving home, and despite the baron's complaints – "Just because I'm old doesn't mean I couldn't whip the hide off you or any other chap, young Victor" – he had hired half a dozen bulky village youths to guard the castle day and night. He was determined that Elizabeth and his father should be safe during his absence. He had been exploring the valley for three weeks now, and at last he was beginning to feel that he had shed some of the misery and guilt he felt about the deaths in Geneva. It was as if there had been a great weight on his shoulders which was slowly being lifted.

In the distance, on the far side of the valley, the slopes of Mont Blanc rose imperiously up to meet the clouds. Just the sight of the huge mountain's icecap was enough to make Victor feel cold. Nearer to him was a smaller mountain – really only a hill – which his map told him was called Montanvert. Its slopes were invitingly green, purple and brown. Victor squinted up at the sun. If he made good progress, he should be able to spend a part of the afternoon exploring the foothills of Montanvert before finding somewhere to stay in the little village he could see down in the valley. Throwing the last of his food to an inquisitive crow, he heaved his knapsack onto his back, grabbed his stick, and set off, singing an old folksong as he navigated his way through the tussocks of the hilly slope.

It took him longer to reach Montanvert than he'd expected, and by the time he came to the summit the afternoon was nearing its end. He began to worry that soon darkness would fall as he turned to make his way back down. Then he noticed that there was someone else on the mountain.

At first the figure was too distant for Victor to be able to make out any details, but as it came closer, he saw that the person was a very large man – too large, Victor began to realize, to be a man at all. It was running across the ground at a colossal speed with a strange mixture of clumsiness and grace. And, though occasionally it had to divert from its path, it was obvious that the figure was heading straight for him.

The creature! It had found him! It must have followed him from the castle.

Victor simply accepted the fact that he was about to die. In a way he almost welcomed it. All the old guilt about the deaths of William and Justine came back to him in a rush. He deserved to die; he had said that to himself time and time again in the darkness of his curtained bedroom. Now that the moment had come, he felt no resentment. It seemed only right and proper that the thing he had created should be the means by which his life ended. He tossed his stick to one side, then chucked his knapsack after it. He sat down on a small hummock and waited calmly for the monster to reach him.

Then his mood changed. He still did not care about dying – although the thought of how unhappy Elizabeth would be made his heart pang – but a bitter hatred of the creature had begun to grow inside him. He knew the hatred was unjustified – if a mad dog kills a child there is no sense in hating the dog – but that didn't make the emotion any less intense. It was not his hands that had tightened around William's small neck. Victor's fury rose. He scrabbled across the hillside to retrieve his stick, the only weapon available to him. He deserved to die – he said this to himself yet again – but so did the monster. If he died killing it, then that was a fair bargain. He clutched his stick and waited impatiently for the monster to reach him.

One moment, it seemed, the creature was still far away; the next it was directly in front of him. Victor looked at it with disgust. It had somehow made clothes for itself out of sheets and blankets. From what he could see of its skin, it looked as if it had been sewn together from old strips of leather of different textures and shades. Its features were enough to spark horror in the strongest mind, as if the various parts of a face – the nose, lips, teeth and cheeks – had been thrown together crazily by a small child. And set in that hideous visage were the being's loathsome eyes, yellow and filled with detestation.

Those eyes were focused on Victor's face.

"You killed them, didn't you?" Victor said.

The creature nodded. It seemed to be merely acknowledging a fact rather than making a confession.

"I wish you were dead," Victor hissed. "I wish you could die more than once – ten times over for each of the innocents whose deaths you caused."

"I expected nothing better from you," said the creature. Victor started. Its voice was a low growl, yet the words were perfectly clear. Where had it learned to speak? The beast spat onto the grass, then warily settled down a few yards away from Victor.

"You created me. Somehow you brought me into this world. You gave me life. And yet, as soon as I was alive, you spurned me because of my appearance. You are my father and my god, but when I was newborn you abandoned me. You gave me legs and arms," – the creature shook its limbs, as if Victor might not have noticed them – "and a heart and lungs and a brain, but then, as I suffered the agony of my birth, you fled from me. What would you say about any other father who abandoned his child at the moment of its birth?"

"You killed my brother," said Victor flatly.

"Yes," said the creature. "I didn't want to kill him. I had no notion of killing him until I tried to make friends with him."

The monster gave a weary sigh. Then it asked:

"Do you want to hear the full tale of what happened since I left Ingolstadt?"

"You may as well tell me," said Victor. "I still want to plunge this stick" – he waved the puny weapon – "into the very depths of your heart, but before I do that I'll listen to your tale."

The monster moved in a blur of speed. Victor found he was no longer holding the stick.

"Listen," said the creature, "listen, you stupid, pathetic little man. Physically I am so much your superior that I could snap you in two at any moment I chose. Mentally, too, I am far in advance of you. In a mere few weeks I have learned to speak – few human children could have done that."

Victor bowed his head. The creature was right.

"But," said the creature, "in other respects I'm still a child. I know what the words 'good' and 'evil' mean, because I've heard them used often enough, but I don't feel them. I didn't feel I was doing anything evil when I was killing your brother – all I knew was that I had to stop him from screaming for help. You gave me a body and a mind, Victor Frankenstein, but you forgot all about giving me a conscience."

"It was an experiment," Victor said limply. "I don't know how I could have given you a conscience. I don't know how I could have given you the power to tell the difference between good and evil. I grew you in a tank of chemicals. That was all I did."

The creature shook with anger, and again Victor assumed he was about to die. Then he saw it force itself to be calm.

"If you had stayed with me in Ingolstadt," it said, "and taught me, like any other father would have done, I might have been able to understand good and evil. But you didn't do that. The first I knew of the world was that my father was screaming because I looked revolting to him."

Victor could think of nothing to say. He had created a being that had a rational mind, but not a soul. It was not the creature that had killed William and Justine, but himself. As twilight fell over the slopes of Montanvert, he began to weep. He had meant no harm, and yet, simply because his creation had been ugly, he had caused so much.

"I offered to tell you my tale," said the creature. "Now I shall do so and you will listen until I'm finished. If you try to leave I'll tear you limb from limb – I swear it."

"I'll listen," said Victor. "It's the least I owe you."

As the sun lowered and the day grew cooler, the monster began to tell its tale . . .

THE MONSTER'S TALE

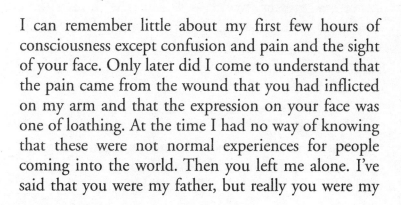

I can remember little about my first few hours of consciousness except confusion and pain and the sight of your face. Only later did I come to understand that the pain came from the wound that you had inflicted on my arm and that the expression on your face was one of loathing. At the time I had no way of knowing that these were not normal experiences for people coming into the world. Then you left me alone. I've said that you were my father, but really you were my mother – it was you who gave me life. When you abandoned me, you were like a mother abandoning her newborn baby. I didn't understand this then, but I do understand it now. Are you surprised I hate you, Frankenstein?

I had some difficulty sorting out my senses. The light shining in through your laboratory windows was so dazzling that I could do nothing except stagger around, my hand across my eyes, hoping for the torment to end. As I did so, I discovered new sources of pain; soon I learned not to tread on the sharp pieces of glass on the floor, but it took me a little longer to discover I should not stumble into the hard corners of your bench or other objects. Every sound was deafening, especially my own screams of anguish. It didn't occur to me that there might be any world outside that room, even though I could hear the noise from the street below.

Then, finally, night came, and with it the gentler moonlight. At last I was able to see. I looked out through the window and discovered that there was indeed a greater world – I saw the houses and buildings of Ingolstadt. At first I didn't know what they were – it was as if I were looking at a flat picture and not understanding what it meant – but then I noticed people with forms much like my own, with two legs and two arms and a head, and I believed that they were just like me. I observed that they wore clothing to cover their bodies, and I hunted around to find similar garments with which I could cover myself. I didn't know why the body should be covered.

I just wanted to
be like those laughing, happy people
I could see from the window. I found some of
your clothes, Frankenstein, but of course none of
them would fit me. In the end I tore the sheets from
your bed and draped them around myself.

I came out into the street, looking for the people I
had seen, but there was no one – only the darkness.
I looked up at the sky and saw the half moon and the

pinpoints of the stars. Here and there were lighted windows, but my mind didn't connect these with living creatures – they could just have been stars that were closer to me than the ones in the sky. Their brightness hurt my eyes. I shambled on clumsily through the streets of Ingolstadt, my sheets gathered pitifully around me, with no idea of where I was going. Eventually I reached the edge of the town, and without hesitation I struck out for the welcome darkness of the countryside.

Other sensations were making themselves felt. I was hungry and thirsty, although at first I didn't know what to do about these aches. I was also exhausted. I lay down by a stream in the middle of the forest, and after a while instinct told me to drink some water. I cupped a little in my hands, and drank. The water tasted so good that I drank more, and more, until I thought my belly would burst. I ate some grass and leaves, and then for some reason I was attracted to the fruits and berries dangling from the trees. I ate a few, and enjoyed their sweetness, so I ate more and more. In the end I was sick, but I soon became hungry and thirsty again. This time I drank and ate more moderately. My appetites satisfied, I curled up under a tree and slept.

I awoke with the dawn. I was freezing cold – though at the time I didn't understand what this meant, or how to make myself warmer. There was a pleasant sound in the air, and after a while I realized that it came from the small, winged creatures darting between the trees. The sunlight no longer stung my eyes: I had become accustomed to the brilliance of day. I drank some more water, ate some more berries, then set off deeper into the countryside.

Several days passed. One day I discovered the remnants of a fire that had been left by some forest folk, and warmed myself in front of it. The fire seemed somehow so friendly that I put my hand into the embers. I discovered at that moment, as you may imagine, Frankenstein, the dual nature of fire. This is one of the many things that you should have taught me, but you chose to desert me instead, because you thought my face was ugly and found me repulsive.

I soon discovered how to keep the fire alight, so I camped there for a few days, sleeping in glorious warmth, then adding fuel and fanning the flames in the morning. The forest folk had left some cooked foods around the fire, which I ate, and then I experimented – finding that heat destroyed berries but made nuts and roots more pleasant to eat. Before long, however, I had eaten everything nearby that seemed edible, and so I resumed my travels.

Soon I came across a mountain hut. I had seen houses in Ingolstadt, of course, but this looked nothing like them – it was all sloping angles and patched walls. I didn't know what it was. I examined it from afar, then opened its door and put my head inside. There was a man there. He took one look at my face and screamed. I backed away, not knowing what a scream was, and he pushed past me and ran away across the fields. I went into the shack and found that he had been eating and drinking substances that I have learned were bread and cheese and milk and wine. I devoured the bread and cheese and milk. The wine tasted disgusting, so I left it. There was a straw bed in the corner, and after my meal I slept for a while.

On waking, I left the hut and continued to walk through the hills. In the evening I came to a village. This was a tiny settlement compared to Ingolstadt, but it seemed almost as grand a place to me. If I'd seen the grandness of Castle Frankenstein by then, I'd have realized that most of the houses were little more than hovels, but at the time I was awed.

I shoved open the door of one of the houses, and at once everyone inside started shrieking. Their noise aroused the other villagers, and I was chased away with sticks and stones. Catching my breath in a field some miles away, I came to the conclusion that I was hideous as well as big. Screams, I had discovered, were the human way of expressing fear or anger. I had no wish to make people scream. I wished no harm on any human being – not yet.

I slept in the field that night, then continued my wanderings in the morning. At about noon I came across an isolated cottage. I crept up close to it. There was smoke coming out of its chimney. On one side of the cottage, leaning against the wall, was a wooden shed. I looked through one of the cottage windows and saw three people gathered around a crudely constructed table. They were eating a meal. My mouth watered as I saw the bread and cheese, but I had learned that other mortals rejected me on sight so I did not knock on the door.

Instead, I investigated the lean-to shed and found that its inside was covered in spiders' webs and filth: it seemed that the place hadn't been used for years. I slipped inside and quietly closed the door behind me. I had found a home. For the first week that I lived there I stayed motionless all day, enjoying the little warmth that filtered through the wall of the cottage. At night, after the dwellers in the cottage had gone to their beds, I went out to find vegetables and hunt down night creatures, which by this time I had discovered were delicious, even when raw.

Once I snatched an owl from the air and gobbled it up on the spot, bones and beak and all.

After a few days I became curious about the people who lived in the cottage. I waited until all of them were out and then, using this fingernail, I gouged a little hole through the wall. From this time onward I was able to watch their daily activity. I learned so much from them! The first thing I learned was speech. It was soon clear to me that the same noises came from their lips each time they referred to an object: a bowl was a concave wooden thing into which food was poured so that someone could eat it using a tool called a spoon. The idea of naming things was new to me; the notion that similar objects could have the same name took me a little longer to master, but at last I had it – one apple could be different from another in size and shape, but both were called apple. In a few more days I was able to comprehend that different actions, too, could be described by sounds. Watching through the hole, I silently repeated each of the sounds I heard the cottagers use. At night, in the open fields, I said the words out loud, over and over again.

I discovered also that these three people had names. The man with the grey hair was called Father. One of the younger people was called Agatha and the other Felix. I knew the two younger people were different in some way, but it was only when I observed them bathing that I was able to know what the difference was. Felix was similar to me; Agatha was not. At the time this discovery was of no more interest to me than the discovery of a new word; it is only recently that I have realized how much I crave someone like Agatha as my partner in life.

I already knew that the three people I loved so much – and I did love them – were extremely unhappy. All of them worked from dawn until darkness, and still they weren't able to get enough food from their fields and traps to fill themselves. And when the weather suddenly got much colder, their life seemed to become even harder.

I did what I could for them. Each night I gathered wood from the forest, and left it in a pile near the cottage. Once I'd satisfied my own hunger, I would catch and kill an extra couple of small animals, and leave them there for my friends. The cottagers were mystified by all this, of course, and at first were unwilling to use the fuel or to eat the hares and birds. Soon, though, they accepted my gifts.

I discovered one more thing about the trio: Father couldn't see. Although he normally moved around the cottage with confidence, he would trip over a chair that had been left in the wrong place or be unable to find a utensil that was not hanging on its customary hook. His children did their best to avoid such situations, but sometimes they forgot.

When I realized the old man was blind, my heart was filled with hope. Other people – including yourself, Frankenstein – had reacted to my appearance with hatred and revulsion. A blind man might accept me for what I was. He would hear my voice – I was now speaking fluently, though my vocabulary was still limited – and assume that I looked much like him. Once he had accepted me, perhaps Agatha and Felix would learn to ignore my face and welcome me into their family.

I was still waiting for a time when Father was alone when a newcomer arrived. Her name was Safie. She was a foreigner, and if anything she was even more beautiful than Agatha. I listened eagerly to the cottagers' conversations over the next few days, and discovered why she was there. Apparently her father had swindled the cottagers a few years before, which was why they were now poverty-stricken. However, Safie and Felix had fallen in love, even though they spoke only a few words in common. Now, at last, she had been able to escape from her father to join her beloved Felix.

She was welcomed by the family. Agatha embraced her as if she were a long-lost sister, and Father didn't stop smiling for days. But it was the way Safie and Felix looked at each other that first informed me of the different sort of love that can exist between two people. Whenever they were together it was as if a cloud of happiness surrounded them. When they were alone they kissed each other.

Soon Father took it upon himself to give Safie daily language lessons and, my eye pressed to the hole in the wall, I learned alongside her – in fact, I took some pride in the fact that I soon raced ahead of her. When you created me, Frankenstein, you gave me a good brain. If only you had known how to give me this thing called a soul which I often heard my cottagers talk about!

One day, when Felix and Safie had gone for a ramble in the countryside and Agatha had gone to a nearby farm to trade some vegetables for eggs, Father remained alone in the cottage. This was my opportunity. I slipped out of my hovel and knocked gently on the front door of the cottage.

"Who's there?" said Father nervously.

"A stranger," I said, as gently as I could. "I'd be grateful if you would allow me to sit by your fire for a few minutes before I continue on my way." I heard him moving inside, then he opened the door.

"Welcome," he said. "Come in."

He gestured to one of the chairs in front of the fire, and settled himself back into the other.

"I am blind," he said immediately. "If you would like some food, please help yourself to whatever you can see. My family will be back soon, and if you can wait, one of them will make you a meal."

I felt a welling up of emotion at his kindness. "I'm not hungry," I said. "But I thank you for your offer."

"Then warm yourself, friend," he said with a smile. He picked up his pipe and lit it with a taper. For a little while neither of us spoke.

"You have a curious accent," he said at last. "Where do you come from?"

"Not far away," I said. There was another silence.

"What brings you to these parts?" he said suddenly.

"I'm looking for a family."

"Would I know them? We haven't lived here very long, but we know some of the people around here." And he tapped his pipe against the cast-iron edge of the hearth.

"All that I can tell you," I said, leaning back in my chair and drawing a deep breath, "is that they're the kindest and gentlest folk I've ever encountered. You cannot see my face, my friend, but it is so grossly ugly that everywhere I go people chase me away. I believe that this family will not." He finished refilling his pipe, and struggled with the business of lighting it again.

"What makes you think that?" he said, when at last the tobacco was glowing.

"I have performed various acts of friendship for them," I said as lightly as I could.

"Then of course they'll welcome you," he cried. "How could they do anything else?"

"They are very poor," I said, plucking up my courage. "The father is blind, and he has a son and a daughter. It is very difficult for them to scratch a living from their land. Just recently they have welcomed into their home an extra person, and that has made it even harder for them to survive."

A frown creased the old man's brow. "It sounds as if you're describing my family," he said slowly.

"I am," I said.

I went down on my knees in front of him. "I've seen the love that the four of you share, and I love you as though I were one of you. I know that I am hideous – every person who has ever looked at me has told me, by their screams, that I am the most repulsive being that has ever stepped upon God's earth. But my heart is pure. I'm your friend. I'm the one who has been stacking up fuel and food outside your door these past weeks. I don't ask for much – no more than a dog would ask – and in return I'll give you everything I can."

Father looked pale. He felt for my hand. "You're far bigger than a normal man," he said tentatively.

"And far, far uglier," I said. My eyes were wet with tears, but I took his hand and put it against my face. "Though you can't see it, you can feel my ugliness."

His fingers explored my features, and he gave a hiss of indrawn breath. Then he took his hand away.

"You are not," he said reflectively, "a handsome man. But Safie's father was handsome, and look at the way he treated me – and her. The outside of a person doesn't tell what the inside of them is like.

I've heard you speak. Everything you've said to me persuades me that your heart is an honest one. We can make a bed of straw here in the main room, and you can live with us."

I kissed his hand, and began to weep out loud. After a moment's hesitation, he put his arm around my shoulder and gave me the kind of hug any parent would give – the kind of hug you have never given me, Frankenstein.

It was at that moment that the door of the cottage flew open and Safie and Felix returned. I looked up. Safie took one glance at me and fainted. Felix gave a shriek of undiluted wrath and snatched a walking stick from beside the door. He took a couple of paces forward and began to beat me about the face.

"What's going on?" shouted Father. "This man is my friend!"

Felix paid him no attention, but continued hitting me with the walking stick. I put up my arms in front of my face to shield myself from the vicious blows.

I could have killed Felix, you know, Frankenstein. It would have been easy for me to pull his body to pieces, to rip his heart from his chest. But instead I merely threw him back against the wall, stunning him. He lay there, breathing heavily.

"I wanted your friendship," I said quietly to the old man, "but it seems there is no one in the world who will be my friend."

"Wait!" he said.

"No," I replied immediately, "I won't wait. Safie fainted when she saw me. Felix attacked me. Would Agatha lose her wits at the sight of my face? I can't risk that. I love you and your family. I wish you well. If ever I come by here again I'll leave a gift on your doorstep, as I have done so often before. But Felix has convinced me that I look too vile to live among ordinary human beings. I must find my own father. He, surely, will accept me for what I am."

In the few moments before you abandoned me in your laboratory, Frankenstein, you mentioned the name "Geneva", and through my eavesdropping on Safie's language lessons, I now knew this was a town somewhere to the north. Using the sun as my guide, I headed north as fast as I could. I had to cross a great mountain range. I discovered that in darkness I could ask people directions – so long as they could not see my face, they assumed that I was just a giant man.

They were only too eager to tell me the route I should take, because they were frightened of my size.

At last, more by luck than judgement, I found myself on the outskirts of Geneva. Huddling at the edge of the lake, the town looked very beautiful. In my innocence I thought that all I would have to do was discover where in Geneva you lived, search you out, introduce myself – and then you would welcome me. What had happened when you first saw me must have been a mistake. Now you would be proud of me. The pain of the rejection I had experienced at the hands of the cottagers was fading: I assumed you would love me, because you were my parent – just as Father loved Agatha and Felix.

I reached Geneva not long after sunset. The town's gates were closed and there were men with metal sticks guarding them. I thought for a moment about beating on the gates and demanding entrance, but then I realized the guards might hurt me. I decided instead to look for somewhere nearby where I could spend the night. Tomorrow would be soon enough to meet you. Had I known you were not there I would have set out for Ingolstadt. But I thought you would be in Geneva, because that is where you had prayed to your God you could be.

In the end I found a cave. I think a bear must have lived there at some time, but it hadn't been used for a long while, and it sheltered me from the night winds. I caught a late-roaming rabbit and ate it. I drank from a stream. Then I went to my cave and lay down, ready for sleep. Sleep was a long time coming. The earth beneath me seemed warm, and yet I was cold. I drifted in and out of dreams until the sunrise, when at last I fell into a deep slumber. When I awoke again it was midafternoon. Somewhere near me I could hear voices. I cowered at the back of my cave, hoping these people, whoever they were, would soon go away. I wanted to catch the moment between dusk and the closing of Geneva's gates when I could enter the town and find where you lived, Frankenstein.

A boy disturbed my plans. He came to the mouth of my cave, and giggled.

"Hello there, Mr. Bear!" he shouted.

I hoped he would run away, but he didn't. Instead he began to come into the cave. If there had been a bear living there he would have been dead within seconds. I gave a growl, hoping that would frighten him off, but he just giggled again. I growled again. Still he came in.

A thought struck me. Adult human beings recoiled from me, but perhaps children would be different. I was like a child myself, and all I could see in the world was beauty – because I was able to see through the outward layer of ugliness that so many things have, and perceive the beauty within. Almost all human adults, I knew, found this impossible. Perhaps children were different. Perhaps this boy would be like me. I got up and moved into the light.

"Hello," I said. He began to retreat.

"There's no need to be frightened," I said. "I won't do you any harm. I'm a friend."

He continued to back away.

"I'm the ugliest man you've ever seen." I laughed. "I'm even uglier than that. But I won't hurt you."

He was still retreating, but more slowly now. Once he was out in the daylight he seemed more confident. In fact, he seemed impatient to see the frightful monster I had described. But when I emerged from the cave, he gave a single shriek and began to run. He kept screaming as he ran. Before I knew what I was doing, I was chasing after him, as if he were one of the hares I had hunted down to give to Father's family. I caught him easily, within seconds.

"I want to be your friend," I said wearily.

He just kept screaming.

"I don't want to hurt you," I repeated, but even as I did so I found that I was picking him up and getting ready to wring his neck, just as I had done countless times before with the wild animals that I'd caught. He screamed even louder. I killed him. It was a reflex. One moment he was alive and the next he was dead. I hurled his small body from me, so that it went tumbling away through the bracken. I squatted down on my haunches and thought . . . nothing. If I'd killed a rabbit I would have felt some satisfaction. Now all that I felt was that I had rid myself of a noisy nuisance. The afternoon was very bright. The songs of the birds were sweet in my ears. The hillside beneath my cave was bare but for bracken.

After a while, I went to look at the corpse of the creature I had killed. Around its neck there was a glittering object that attracted my attention. I snapped the chain and examined this thing. I put it in my mouth and pressed my teeth against it, thinking it might be food; but it tasted horrible. Looking at it more closely, I discovered there was a clasp on one side. When I pressed this, the object fell open at a hinge, and I found myself looking at a picture of you, my dear Herr Frankenstein.

There was another picture inside the frame. It showed the face of a woman. I had believed that there could be no woman more beautiful than Safie, but I was wrong. This woman had ringlets of gold falling around a face of such exquisite loveliness that it drove the breath from my body. Ah, Frankenstein, you have already told me her name. Elizabeth. It is a name that I'll remember. I can see from your face that you love this Elizabeth, and I loved her picture.

I left the boy's body where it was, but took the locket away with me. I felt no guilt about having killed him, as I say, but I knew that other human beings would wish to seek revenge for what I had done. I had to make myself scarce for at least a few days – perhaps a few weeks. I also realized that by killing someone close to you, Frankenstein – though at the time I had no idea that this was your brother – I had almost certainly earned your hatred.

Up until that moment, I had been prepared to forgive you everything. Through my observations of the cottagers, I had discovered the love that people could share – Father had loved his children, and they had loved him, even though his blindness made him a burden on them. I had been ready to love you, because you were my parent. But now – now that I knew you would hate me – I began to reflect upon the evil that you had done to me.

You had brought me into this world, which was crime enough, but then, seeing that your unnatural offspring was less pretty than other men, you just abandoned me. I began to understand that killing a child was a sin, but it was something that would never have happened had you treated me like a son, like any other father would.

Hours passed, and night fell. I moved around the hillside in the moonlight. All thoughts of entering Geneva and finding you had ebbed. I tell you, Frankenstein, by now I hated you. It must have been after midnight when I discovered a barn. My steps quickened. I could sleep in the straw, and then leave in the morning before the farmer was up and about.

But I found someone else already sleeping there – a young woman.

You gave me a mind and a brain, Frankenstein; you also gave me slyness. I looked at the locket I still clutched in my hand, and I looked at the sleeping woman. Carefully, making no noise, I tucked the locket into the pocket of her outer garment.

She snored abruptly on feeling my touch, and turned over. I moved to the door, but she didn't wake up. When I was certain that she was still deeply asleep, I climbed a ladder into the upper loft. There I settled myself in the hay, and at last sleep came.

Later I heard that they had hanged the woman who was in the barn. If I were a human, I wouldn't have hanged her, even if I'd known she was guilty. Think of it – if she had been guilty, which of course she wasn't, of killing your brother, the only reason could have been that she was sick in her mind. Do you humans hang people because they're sick? It appears you do, because you hanged this woman.

One of the things I discovered while I was observing the cottagers was that it was evil for human beings to kill each other – or harm each other in any way. You humans say these things, and yet you then go out and do exactly the opposite.

I don't have any such feelings about guilt or innocence, Frankenstein. As I said, I felt no more emotion over killing your brother than I would if I'd killed a hare. I could kill you right now if I wanted to. Don't jerk away like that. You're safe enough. For my own purposes I want to keep you alive.

I saw the emotion that existed between Felix and Safie. A little while ago, when I mentioned Elizabeth's name, I could see in your face the emotion you feel for her. It is an emotion that I wish I could share. And yet what mortal woman would look at me without revulsion? You made me, Frankenstein. You brought me into the world. It is your duty to provide a mate for me, a female who is like myself. A woman who will look at me with the same softness in her eyes that Safie had when she looked at Felix.

If you create a mate for me, I will leave your life forever. Once we are united, we will find somewhere far away from any human contact, and live our lives there and you will never hear from me again. If you refuse to do this, then all of your family and loved ones are at risk. I shall pick them off one by one. You love Elizabeth. It's obvious every time I mention her name. You plan to marry her.

Listen to me, Frankenstein, and listen well. Unless you do what I want – unless you create a bride for me – then I shall be with you on your wedding night!

THE BRIDE

The creature beat the fist of one hand into the palm of the other with each of its final words. Then it sprang up, and in an instant was sprinting away down the side of Montanvert. Though the moonlight was bright, Victor lost sight of the beast almost immediately. With a heavy heart, he pulled himself to his feet and began the long trudge down the mountain to the village he had seen that morning.

Create another monster? A female? How would he go about it? He could hardly ask Elizabeth to allow him to gouge a strip of flesh from her body. And anyway, he wasn't sure if he wanted to run the risk of creating another murderous monster. Yet the creature had said that it would be out of his life forever if he agreed to its demand – that it and its mate would avoid any contact with the human race.

He was lucky to find the last available bed in an inn that night, but he couldn't sleep. All night long he wrestled with his dilemma. It was only when the first light of the morning reached in through the curtains to touch the end of his bed that he was able to come to a conclusion.

The monster was right. It had been treated abominably throughout its short existence. If a mate would bring it happiness, then a mate it should have. Oddly enough, its threat to continue its campaign of murder had little bearing on Victor's decision. He splashed some water in his mouth, shivering in the cold air. His eyes felt gritty. Minutes later he paid his bill and set off for Geneva.

Once back at home, however, Victor found himself procrastinating. He would have to set up his new laboratory in secret, and this was something he found almost impossible to arrange. If Henry – who had just arrived from Ingolstadt and was staying at the castle during his annual vacation from the university – was not by his side, then Elizabeth was, and if not Elizabeth, the baron. And the old man had become so aged by the deaths of William and Justine that he needed a supporting shoulder simply to move from one room to the next.

With just over a month left until their planned wedding date, Victor told Elizabeth that he had to go away again.

"I have more scientific research to do," he said sadly. They were eating breakfast together. His father and Henry had yet to emerge from their bedrooms.

She put her hand on his. "Must you go?" she said.

"Yes. I'd rather spend the time away from home now than after we're married, dear Elizabeth."

"Where will you go?"

"England. There are libraries in London that contain books and treatises which are unavailable here. All the time I was at Ingolstadt I was frustrated by the lack of the books I needed. If I don't go to London now to consult them, I'll be unable to tear myself away from you for years, perhaps forever."

"We could wait until after the wedding," she said, "and then go to England as man and wife."

"It would be tedious for you, Elizabeth," he said. "All day long I'd be closeted away in the library, and all night long I'd be doing my calculations. No, it's much better if I go now."

Her face softened. "If you really think that would be the best thing, Victor . . ."

"I do."

A few minutes later Henry appeared.

"You two look as if you've been talking far too seriously for a morning as beautiful as this one," he said cheerfully, helping himself to some breakfast from the sideboard.

"Victor says he must go to England for a few weeks to continue his research," said Elizabeth, her voice low.

"England!" said Henry, joining them at the table. "What a capital idea! I'll come along, Victor, to keep you on the straight and narrow." He winked at Elizabeth. "I've heard tales about those English girls, you know. Worse than the ones at Ingolstadt, if such a thing could be possible."

Elizabeth giggled.

Victor made a feeble attempt at laughter. "I'd rather go alone, Henry," he said. "I've such a lot to do that I don't want to be distracted." Even as he said the words, he knew they were futile. And after a few more minutes it had been settled. Henry would be accompanying him to England.

The following night Victor crept out of Castle Frankenstein. There was hardly any moon, and the sky was piercingly clear. He turned the collar of his coat up around his ears and blew into his hands, then slipped quietly away across the lawn.

The baron had insisted that Justine be buried in the family plot, which was at the far end of the estate. It took Victor about fifteen minutes to reach it. He was out of view of the house, now, so he took a little lantern from his pocket and, after much difficulty and not a little cursing, got the thing lit. It hardly seemed to produce enough light for his purposes, but he was able to find the spade he had hidden in the corner.

Justine's gravestone was a simple one. Best not to think about what he was going to do. He gave one last anguished glance at the brilliantly twinkling stars, and then thrust the blade of the spade deep down into the earth.

The digging was easier than he had anticipated, and in less than half an hour he had exposed the top of Justine's coffin. He paused to catch his breath. He estimated it would take at least another hour to dig all around the edges of the coffin so that he could lever the lid off. He had to find a quicker way. The silence of the night was oppressive: he wished an owl would hoot or a night creature scream.

Raising the spade high above his head, he brought the edge of the blade crashing down onto the coffin lid. The wood cracked. Again he smashed the spade down, and the crack widened. He stabbed the tip of the spade into the crack, and pushed down with all his might. Splinters flew up. One nearly hit him in the eye. Breathing loudly, he pushed down once again, and this time the wood split open.

A waft of decay erupted from the coffin, drowning the smell of the newly dug earth. Victor gagged. The face he could see dimly in the lamplight was like a hideous parody of the Justine he had known. All the beauty had been stripped away from her. Her lips were drawn back tightly against her teeth, which were set in a terrible grin. Her eyes had rotted away entirely, leaving only empty sockets: at least she wouldn't be able to see what he was about to do. As he watched, a pallid fat worm crept from her nostril and slithered into the darkness below.

"Don't think about it!" he told himself soundlessly.

"Just do it. Do it, then cover her up again and get away from here."

Forcing himself not to remember Justine as a person, he drew a scalpel from his pocket. Keeping his stomach under control with difficulty, he darted the knife forward and stabbed it into Justine's cheek. The flesh came away easily. He hacked two slices from her jaw and clumsily stuffed them into a bag he had brought along for the purpose. "None of this is hurting Justine," he told himself firmly. "She has long departed this corpse. I'm only taking a little of her dead flesh". Even so, he felt his stomach churn again. He vaulted up out of the hole and ran for the wall of the little cemetery. Leaning over it, he vomited violently into the darkness.

Several minutes later, his stomach still rebelling, he forced himself to go back to Justine's graveside. He'd planned to repair the coffin lid as best he could, but he no longer had the heart for that. Weeping bitterly, he hurled the earth back over the face, wielding the spade vigorously in the vain hope that the physical effort would somehow blot out the memory of what he'd just done.

When he'd finished, he sat for a long time on the wall. The leathery strips of Justine's flesh were a guilty weight in his pocket. The lantern's light seemed very small against the ponderous darkness of the night. At last he was able to stop the trembling of his limbs. He hid the spade back in the corner of the plot. Once he was in sight of the castle, its great bulk a smudge against the stars, he blew out his lantern. He was able to get back to his bedroom without being observed, and spent another sleepless night.

In London Victor made a great show of going to all the public libraries, including the Reading Room of the British Museum, which he had heard about but which was far more impressive than he had ever believed possible. Henry tagged along with him for the first few days, but soon became bored. Victor leafed through various books rather aimlessly, pretending to conduct his medical research and, every now and then, coming across something that might help him in the construction of the monster's mate. What he really needed to do, he knew, was order all his chemical supplies and find somewhere he could use as a laboratory, but this was impossible with Henry always in attendance.

After a week or so Victor announced that he had exhausted the resources of London and would now have to head north, to the Royal Library of Scotland, in Edinburgh. He had hoped that Henry would decide to leave him at this point, but the man insisted on accompanying him. He began to hate his old friend. Several more days were wasted as they journeyed north. In Edinburgh Victor spent a day at the Royal Library, then told Henry that his researches required him to travel even farther north.

"There's a library in the Orkney Islands," Victor

lied, "that may contain the final clue. The Orkneys are far to the north of the northernmost point of Scotland, dear friend, and the sea crossing is often rough. I can't drag you there, Henry – you have been far too kind already in accompanying me this far. Besides, your new term at Ingolstadt starts next week. Surely you should be heading for home?"

They'd climbed the hill called Arthur's Seat that morning, and were looking out over the city.

"I worry about you, Victor."

"I can manage, Henry."

Victor said the words with enough determination that his friend stared at him, even more concerned than before.

"Are you sure?"

"I'm absolutely sure. When you get back to Castle Frankenstein, tell Elizabeth that I'll be with her as soon as I can. If it means our marriage must be delayed – well, Henry, until this line of research is complete I'd be unable to settle down."

"Can't you at least tell me what it is you're trying to discover, Victor?"

"Not yet, Henry. Not for a while yet. It's important work, and I don't want anyone else to hear about it. It may come to nothing, of course. And anyway, you probably wouldn't understand it if I tried to explain – I'm afraid that's one of the disadvantages of a classical education, Henry!"

Victor laughed. After a moment, Henry joined in.

The next morning Henry – still offering to stay with Victor if he could be of help – set off for Leith to embark for the continent.

At last Victor was free! He went to the largest apothecary shop in Edinburgh's Princes Street and placed an order for all the chemicals he required. Less then fifty yards away, in Rose Street, he found a builder who was willing to make a tank like the one that Victor had constructed in Ingolstadt. Most important of all was the mountain of electrical batteries he bought, each weighing so much that he had difficulty carrying even one of them.

He had told Henry he must go to the Orkneys only to make his friend leave, but he had since come to the conclusion that the Orkneys were as good a place as anywhere to create the monster's bride. He paid for all the equipment in cash, plus an extra fee to have them delivered to Kirkwall, in the Orkney Islands. That night he set off.

A few days later, Victor waited impatiently by the quay for the boat that was bringing his equipment from Kirkwall. The grey sea churned beneath him, as if it wanted to devour the land. He had at last found himself somewhere that he could set up a new laboratory – the tiny island of Sibbens. It was little more than a rock jutting up out of the sea, with sparse patches of grass and wiry vegetation on which a few sheep miserably fed. Apart from the one that he had rented, there were only two other cottages on the island, and the families that lived in them showed hardly any interest in the curious-looking southern stranger with his weird accent. And that was exactly the way he wanted things to remain. He kicked his toe against a crack in the stones of the quay. Would the blasted boat never turn up?

And then finally he saw it, tossing through the angry waters. Within a few minutes, half a dozen friendly sailors were climbing up beside him, and not long after they were carrying the tank and all his various jars and bottles and batteries up the dirt track to the cottage. They had brought his supplies of food and wine as well – enough to keep him going for at least a two weeks, although he planned to stay no more than one. Victor gave them a generous tip and a bottle of brandy to share between them. They shouted their good wishes across the churning sea as the boat retreated into the drab evening.

Victor worked late that night. First he assembled the tank, then he began the slow task of pouring the chemicals into it. The cottage had a fireplace, but he had forgotten to gather any wood or to buy any peat to burn. He was hardly aware of the cold, however, as he toiled feverishly on into the night.

It must have been about five in the morning when finally the concoction of chemicals was mixed. The lamp was flickering, and he added some more oil to it. He gathered together the empty jars.

"I'm simply putting off the moment," he said to himself angrily. "The quicker you get this infernal business started, Victor Frankenstein, the quicker it'll be over. You've done it before, so you can do it again. And then you can go back to Elizabeth and forget all about this miserable period of your life."

He dug out the cloth wallet in which he had brought the scraps of Justine's flesh. They no longer seemed to be remotely human – or even flesh at all. They were just two . . . things. They could have been anything.

"Do it. Do it now."

He tossed the blackened, twisted shreds into the tank. Then, gingerly, he wired the huge batteries together one by one. Finally he dropped the free end of the last wire into the liquid. There was a short-lived blaze of violent light. Then, abruptly, the batteries went dead. But he knew that the electrical charge had been delivered.

He sat back to watch. And nothing happened. Of course nothing would. It would be hours before the flesh began to respond to the nutrients in the tank. He hadn't been able to watch the first of his creatures grow, and he took a sick satisfaction from the fact that this time he would be able to observe how the process progressed. But there would be nothing for him to see in what remained of the night. He threw himself down on a heap of clothing in the corner, and fell asleep at once.

It was well past noon when he awoke, and he spent some moments wondering where on earth he could be. The wind was howling around the little cottage, making the roof grunt and groan as if it wanted to fly away from the walls. The breeze coming in through the hut's ill-fitting door was slowly flicking over the pages of one of Victor's notebooks on the floor.

He sat up stiffly, staring balefully at the pile of empty jars. He would have to get rid of them all somehow, he supposed. It was only then that he thought to turn his attention to the contents of the tank.

The two leathery strips of flesh had come together, but that wasn't the first thing he noticed. What was most obvious was the way that they had changed. Where before they'd been blackened by decay, now they were a strange, shining pink. He remembered how his creature had seemed at first – as if it had been flayed – before contact with the air had hardened its skin. It looked as if the same would be true of the ghastly bride.

He peered more closely through the glass. The flesh had grown during the time that he had been asleep.

Already it was at least three times the size that it had been when he had thrown its component pieces into the liquid. Swirls of what appeared to be blood hung in the clear fluid around it. All thoughts of the morality of what he was doing fled. He was amazed and fascinated. He watched the tank for an hour or more, telling himself he could see minor changes taking place, before hunger forced him away. Even then, as he ate an unpalatable meal of stale bread and over-ripe cheese, he continued to stare at the tank.

Days passed, and the flesh continued to expand. He had half-expected that it would form itself into a perfect miniature of a human being, and then simply increase in size; or, perhaps, it might go through all the stages his medical textbooks had shown him of the developing baby in the womb. In fact, it did neither. There seemed no pattern at all to its changes. The first recognizably human part of it to appear was an arm. Then from the end of this sprang – with shocking swiftness – the right-hand side of a ribcage, over which the flesh crept so quickly that Victor could almost see its progress.

In this unpredictable fashion, the creature grew, until at last there came a morning when it had the first semblance of a face.

At which point, all Victor's earlier qualms returned. It was too soon to be certain, but the rudimentary features looked horribly like Justine's. He ran out of the hut, slamming the door behind him. It was all he could do not to scream.

The wind-borne rain was like a bitterly cold hand slapping his face. Hunching his shoulders, he pressed on through it, to the sea. The sky was dark grey, and seemed so heavy that it was barely able to support itself. The little island had never appeared so desolate or hostile.

He kicked among the pebbles along the shore. He hadn't expected the she-monster he was creating to look anything like Justine – after all, the original beast had looked nothing like himself. Or had it? He had left the monster in the tank in Ingolstadt far longer than his calculations had indicated he should. Had it, at one stage during its development, resembled himself, Victor Frankenstein, exactly, and then continued to grow until it became horrific?

But there were more urgent matters to consider. If the bride he was growing for her fearful mate looked like Justine, might she not have all of Justine's sensibilities? Would she resemble the dead woman in mind as much as in physical appearance? If that were the case, how could he think of handing her over to the frightful being who had killed Victor's younger brother and who had caused the death of Justine herself? Would she be willing to live out the rest of her life in some remote corner of the world, with no one else to share her existence except a creature so vile that no one could look at it without a shudder? Could he condemn Justine – poor, sweet, innocent Justine – to an existence like that?

At the same time, could he deny the female creature life? The real Justine could never live again – the hangman's noose had seen to that – but the replica Victor was growing would also, surely, seek to live. Did he have the right to deny it – her – that privilege?

He remembered Justine all too vividly. She had been a person who was vibrant with the joy of living. In part he had been responsible for her death. Could he take away her life a second time? All day he walked along the rainswept shore, circling the little island several times, deaf to the pounding of the sea against the boulders. As night fell, he groped his way back to the hut, his heart leaden. He knew what he must do.

As soon as he was inside, he threw off his soaking coat and lit the lamp. Not giving himself any more time to think, he lashed out with his boot at the side of the tank, and the glass shattered. A torrent of liquid flooded out over his legs, drenching him to the knees before it gurgled out through the gap under the door.

Then he seized two of his scalpels. Kicking aside the broken glass, he reached through and grabbed the shoulder of the partial corpse, dragging the heavy flesh out onto the stone floor, where it flopped with a revolting noise. He raised his right hand and plunged a scalpel into the partly formed chest of the dead creature, ripping down to the torso. Blood – human blood, or an approximation of it – sprayed everywhere.

Victor turned his face away. He felt as if he were killing Justine all over again, even though the carcass he was attacking had not yet attained the spark of life. When he looked back, the eyes had opened with a terrible look of alarm. Justine's clear eyes looked directly into his. She was trying to scream in agony, but her vocal cords had not yet formed.

He froze. Those eyes were imploring him to stop.

But Victor made himself continue. He told himself that the opening of the eyes was merely a reflex brought about by severing a nerve. The dead meat could not possibly be conscious. He slashed again with the scalpels, first one and then the other, ripping the half-formed creature to pieces. He never knew just how long this act of imitation murder took him. It could have been five minutes or it could have been an hour. In the end he stumbled back from the evidence of his butchery and cowered against the wall, curling up into a ball, unwilling to confront the true horror of what he had done.

And still the wind – the relentless, pitiless Orkney wind – screeched around the cottage. Drenched in blood, Victor was shaking with terror.

Then, all at once the gale dropped. In the silence, there was a tap at the window opposite him. Once more, Victor froze. Then, both dreading and knowing what he might see, he slowly raised his eyes. Pressed against the outside of the glass, was a huge hand – the monster's hand. Even through the dirty glass, he could see that the features of its face were grossly distorted.

"I will seek revenge, Frankenstein!" it bellowed. "I will seek revenge on you and all whom you hold dear!"

Then the creature was gone. How long had it been watching him? Terrified and remorseful, Victor curled up even smaller.

The tempest returned.

WEDDING NIGHT

Somehow Victor slept, and in the morning he felt as if many of the cares of his life had somehow been lifted from his shoulders. Before last night he'd been terrified of the creature; now, once again, he had returned to a state of mere acceptance of his doom. He almost looked forward to death.

Setting to work methodically, he cleaned his scalpels and stowed them away in his case. Most of his clothes were filthy, but he folded them roughly and packed them away as well. He couldn't do much about the wreckage of the tank, or the countless glass jars that were scattered everywhere, but he certainly had to get rid of the remains of the half-formed Justine. Taking care not to spatter his clean clothes with blood, he packed the pieces of flesh into an old canvas bag along with some heavy stones. This done, he mopped the floor, trying to get rid of all traces of blood.

He knew he had to get away from the island. Where he was going to go he had no idea, but he wanted to put as much distance between him and the creature as possible. How it had reached the island was something else he didn't know. It must have swum from the mainland. He tried to put out of his mind any thoughts of how far it could swim. He knew there was nowhere on earth he could be safe from it. It would follow him. It had greater speed, strength and stamina than any normal human being.

He trudged across the thin grass to the hovel where the nearest family lived. This family survived mainly on the fish they caught in the chilly waters of the North Sea. Not long ago they had somehow managed to obtain a new boat, but Victor had seen the old one still at anchor, apparently seaworthy.

"What is it that you'd be wanting to buy a boat for?" said the old fisherman, opening his door only the width of his face.

"I want to leave the island. Today."

"But the mailboat will be here early next week," said the fisherman.

"I have to leave before then. Name me a price for the boat."

The old man considered for a moment, then looked up at Victor slyly. "I canna let you have it for less than fifteen pounds," he said.

"Fifteen pounds!" said Victor immediately. "Done!" Then, feeling guilty, he added: "Call it twenty."

"Guineas," said the fisherman, obviously realizing that he was driving a poor bargain.

Victor plucked the coins from his pouch and counted them into the man's hands. "And here's an extra shilling for one of your lads to row me out to it tonight," he said.

The old man was testing the coins between his teeth. "Ay," he said, "tonight."

Victor suddenly understood that the man assumed he was a smuggler. Well, let him think that. The cargo he was going to carry was far more ghastly than anything the fisherman could imagine.

"Tonight," said Victor. "As soon as the moon rises I will be gone from here."

For once the sea wasn't too rough. The fisherman's son dourly waved farewell to Victor in the moonlight and was soon heading back to shore. Victor waited a little while, feeling as if he had just escaped from prison, and then set the boat's single sail. The night was clear, and he was able to get an approximate bearing from the pole star. As long as he plotted a course that was more or less due southeast he would come, sooner rather than later, to Denmark or Germany. There he would abandon the boat and make his way across country by rail or carriage to Geneva. There was one more thing that he must do.

He took hold of the bag containing the remains of the second Justine. As he propped it on the rail he once again imagined he heard the real Justine's laughter as she played with William. He had loved her almost as much as he had loved his brother – indeed, had it not been for Elizabeth, he might well have fallen in love with her. But the travesty of her that had begun to grow in his tank – that was something

best forgotten, best disposed of.
He shoved the bag into the inky waters.
It sank with hardly a bubble. Then,
trusting that the wind would not
change during the night, he went
back below and settled himself on
a dirty bunk.

Three weeks later he was in
Geneva. Elizabeth met him as his
carriage hurtled up the drive to
Castle Frankenstein. She threw
herself into his arms, covering his
face with kisses. At last she pulled
herself away, holding him at arm's length.

"Elizabeth," he said. "Oh, Elizabeth, you
don't know what I've been through. Just seeing your
face again makes me believe there's some hope in life
after all."

Her features clouded. "Not all my news is good,
Victor. Come inside. Let the servants deal with your
luggage. Here, I'll take your coat."

He followed her to a little sitting room just off the
hall. She bustled around for a minute or two, talking
of nothing much, obviously trying to compose herself
for what she really wanted to say. Finally she sat down
in the chair opposite his.

"Your father is very ill," she said, leaning forward
earnestly, her eyes fixed unwaveringly on his. "Very ill
indeed. He's an old man, Victor, and I don't think he's
long for this world."

Victor drew in his breath, then slowly let it out again. "As you say, Elizabeth, he's an old man – and recently he's had to cope with far too much grief. It's not entirely unexpected. I must go and see him."

He half-rose, but Elizabeth gestured to him to remain seated.

"There's one other bit of bad news that I haven't dared tell him yet," she said. Her eyes fell, and she began to pick at a nonexistent loose thread on her skirt. "It's about Henry."

"What's he done?" said Victor.

"Nothing – and he never will again."

"He's dead?"

"Yes."

"But – but what happened?"

She looked up again, and her eyes were full of tears. "He was most brutally murdered. Strangled in Ingolstadt. A week ago. The police believe he was killed by the same person who slew poor William, and they've issued a posthumous pardon to Justine. It was then they discovered that her grave had been desecrated. They dug down to the coffin so the pastor could sprinkle holy water on her and found the coffin lid smashed and Justine's face scored by a knife."

Victor felt as if he couldn't breathe. Henry was dead! The abhorrent monster had returned to Geneva and had started to carry out its threat of destroying all those dear to Victor. He wondered who would be next. His father? Elizabeth? Victor wished that it could be himself, so that there would be an end to the story, but he knew that the creature wasn't able to show such mercy.

He put his face in his hands. "This is terrible," he muttered. "Terrible."

Elizabeth reached out and put her hand on his arm. For a long time they remained motionless. Finally Victor shook his shoulders and stood up. "I must go and see my father," he said. "You were right not to tell him about these dreadful things. He has no need to know. I'll keep them from him as well."

"I'll come with you," she said, gathering up her skirt and standing. "Here, Victor, take my hand."

As they climbed the long curve of the main stairway she added: "And remember, Victor, we must look cheerful for him. After all, you're home safely. Isn't that a cause for celebration?"

Although Elizabeth had half-prepared him, Victor was still shocked by his father's appearance. It seemed the baron had aged ten years or more in the few weeks Victor had been away. He looked not so much old as dead, though still breathing. The flesh of his face had shrunk and grown thinner, so that it was wrapped tightly around his skull. His remaining tufts of white hair looked as if they would break at a touch. His cheeks were craters. His eyes, when he opened them as Victor and Elizabeth entered, looked infinitely tired.

He raised his head from the pillow. "Victor," he

wheezed weakly. "You're home, my boy. Thank God for having preserved you!" Tears glistened at the corners of his eyes.

Victor, recalling how his father's voice had boomed along the corridors in days gone by, knelt by the bed overwhelmed with emotion and kissed the baron's bony hand.

"Yes, father," he said, "I'm home. I wish, seeing you so unwell, I'd come home earlier."

"Nonsense, Victor. There's nothing wrong with me that a few more days in bed won't cure."

Victor could find nothing to say. Then his father sighed deeply. "That was a lie. You know it and I know it, and dearest Elizabeth, who has nursed me more than I deserve, knows it. I'm dying, my son. Who knows whether it'll be days or weeks or . . ."

His voice faded away. Victor stayed on his knees by the bed. The baron laid a hand on his shoulder.

"There is one thing that would make me very happy before I die," the old man said. His voice was as quiet as a soft breeze rustling autumn leaves. "It would be to see you and my darling Elizabeth married at last."

Victor bowed his head. Again, conflicting emotions ran around his brain. He wanted more than anything to please his father. He wanted more than anything to marry Elizabeth. But he also remembered a hoarse voice bawling at him: "I shall be with you on your wedding night!"

"Don't worry, father. We'll be married as soon as the pastor will permit," he said, beginning to sob. When he looked up, his father's eyes had closed once more. But there was a faint hint of a smile on his face.

A week later Victor stood in the doorway of the village church with his new bride leaning against his shoulder. Though thoughts of the creature were never far from his mind, he couldn't help smiling as he leaned over and kissed Elizabeth and heard the cheers of a small crowd of villagers and servants.

It was a gloriously bright morning. The sky was a brilliant alpine blue, with wisps of clouds scurrying high above. Victor couldn't help feeling happy. Two servants carried his father on a chair out from the little chapel and down the porch steps to join him and Elizabeth.

The old man was weeping. "This is the day I've dreamed about for years," he managed to say. "The two people I love most in the world . . ."

He broke off in a fit of coughing. Elizabeth took his face between her hands and kissed him on the forehead. "Now I can truly call you 'father' at last," she said softly.

A carriage was waiting just outside the church grounds, ready to take Victor and Elizabeth to Lake Geneva. They were to honeymoon in Italy – at the Villa Lavenza, on the shores of Lake Como. Today they were going to sail to Evian, where they would spend their first night as man and wife. Tomorrow they would travel on by carriage. Victor felt very relieved that they were putting a great deal of water between themselves and Geneva. Although he knew that the enormous creature was able to swim great distances – his experience in the Orkneys had proved that – the wide lake nevertheless seemed to offer them some sort of security.

The little vessel scudded along, a fresh wind filling the sails. On one side of them Victor and Elizabeth could see Mont Salève, with the huge mass of Mont Blanc in the distance. On the other there were the even more forbidding slopes of the Jura Mountains.

Sometimes he and Elizabeth chattered to each other; other times, trying to ignore the amused eye of the skipper, they kissed.

As evening came they approached Evian. They sent their baggage on to their inn, and spent an hour or two rambling along the beach in the dusk. It was the first time they had been alone since swearing their marriage vows. Elizabeth was becoming happier and happier with each passing moment, but Victor's mood sank. The creature had pledged vengeance upon him. Earlier in the day he had been content to believe that they were too far away for the monster to carry out its threat of being with him on his wedding night; now he became convinced that it would indeed appear.

"What's the matter, Victor?" said Elizabeth.

"I'll tell you tomorrow. There's something dreadful I have to tell you – but it can wait until tomorrow."

"Tell me now," she insisted, clutching his arm.

"Tomorrow."

"You're just teasing." She began to laugh, but then stopped. "Is it something very dreadful, Victor?"

His silence gave her the answer.

"Is it anoth . . . ?"

"No, it's nothing like that," he snapped. Then he was immediately contrite. "Oh, I'm sorry. I shouldn't have spoken to you so sharply. My researches have made me do some very foolish things. Nobody else but me knows what they are. Now that you're my wife, then I must obviously open my heart to you. But I don't want to do that today – today of all days. Let's go to our inn. I'm hungry."

After they'd eaten they sat outside for a long while, watching the town of Evian quieten for the night. One by one, the lighted windows around them darkened. The reflections of the stars shone on the calm waters of the lake. Elizabeth was wearing a shawl, but eventually she shivered inside it. "It's time to go up to bed, Victor," she said shyly. "I'll call you when I'm ready."

She pecked him briefly on the cheek, and was about to leave the terrace when he caught her hand and pulled her back for a long, lingering kiss.

"Don't be long," he said, his voice faltering.

"I won't be," she said, and was gone.

As soon as she'd disappeared, his attention returned to the lake. There was enough moonlight for him to be able to see its mirrored surface stretching all the way to the horizon. If the creature really were swimming to Evian, pursuing them, Victor would be able to spot the splashing a mile away. But all he could see were the occasional expanding rings of ripples where fish jumped or water birds moved.

He clenched the arm of his chair tightly. "I shall be with you on your wedding night," the creature had said savagely. Well, Victor was ready for it. He felt the pistol tucked into his inner jacket pocket – keeping its presence a secret from Elizabeth had been difficult, both when it was in their shared trunk and, after dinner, when he'd slipped it into the pocket. He was also wearing a sword, which he had claimed he'd put on as part of his formal dress for dinner. Little did Elizabeth realize that this was no ceremonial weapon

but the sharpest blade Victor had been able to find
hanging on the walls of Castle Frankenstein. He
waited, motionless, his eyes intently scanning the
surface of the lake. Everyone in Evian had long ago
gone to bed. He was utterly alone.

The night was growing very chilly, but still he kept
up his watch. He was ready for a final confrontation
with the monstrous being he had created. If he could,
he would persuade it to leave him and his dear ones
alone forever; but he was prepared to kill it outright,
if need be. Once again he felt the pistol. Its weight,
under his shoulder, was reassuring.

What was taking Elizabeth so long to prepare for bed? His head began to loll onto his chest as tiredness overtook him.

Then he started. Somewhere above him there had been a shriek and then the sound of a window breaking. Elizabeth!

Something heavy dropped from an upper floor of the inn and lumbered off rapidly through the empty streets. Victor threw himself from his chair and charged into the inn. He leapt up the stairs, repeating over and over again, "No . . . no . . . no!"

He kicked open the door of their room. The first thing he saw was the shattered window. Then his eyes turned to the bed. "Elizabeth!" he screamed. "Oh my God! What have I done to you?"

The bedding was a mass of blood. Elizabeth's body lay across it, her head twisted at an unnatural angle. There was a gaping, gory hole in her chest. On her face – her dead face – there was a look of shock and agony. Her eyes, wide open, seemed to be staring at Victor accusingly. Through the window, from far in the distance, came a maniacal laugh.

Victor threw himself across the body of his dead wife, screamed again, then began to weep. He touched her blonde head tenderly. "Oh, God, Elizabeth, I'm so sorry," he said, although he could hardly see her any longer. "It's my fault, my fault, my fault . . ."

Then there were hands on his shoulders, pulling him away from Elizabeth's corpse. In fits and starts he heard voices. Some of the other guests, woken by his screams, assumed he was Elizabeth's killer and wanted to hang him from the nearest tree. But soon more rational people intervened. Someone guided him to a chair, where he sat sobbing uncontrollably. Another hand offered him brandy, but he was shaking so violently that he was unable to grip the glass.

"Hang me!" he said. "I killed her! It's because of me that she's dead!"

"That's enough of that talk," said a gruff voice. "You weren't the one who escaped through that window, and you weren't the one who took her heart with you." Victor convulsed in even deeper grief. Her heart! The monster might as well have stolen her soul – his soul. Abruptly he stopped weeping, and sat up straight in the chair.

"I know who her murderer is," he said. "I have seen the face of the one who killed her. I will follow this vile criminal to the ends of the earth, and then have my vengeance."

"He's babbling," said someone.

"Wait," said someone else. Victor recognized the voice of the innkeeper. The man bent down to look him in the eyes. "Did you see the murder?"

"No," responded Victor, "but I do know who committed it. There is someone who swore he would wreck my wedding night."

"You can't leave tonight," said the innkeeper. "Someone has sent for the police. They'll want to speak to you. Arrangements must be made for . . . well, arrangements."

"Leave me alone with her," said Victor. "I want to

beg her forgiveness. If it hadn't been for my own stupidity she wouldn't have died like this."

They left him with Elizabeth until the police arrived. For most of the rest of the night he was interviewed, but at last the inspector declared himself satisfied that Victor was innocent. Then the innkeeper took him away into another bedroom, fed him a sedative despite his protestations, and put him into bed.

"I will follow her murderer to the ends of the earth," repeated Victor.

It was the last thing he said before sleep engulfed him.

AMONG THE SNOWS

Captain Walton, skipper of the *Margaret Saville*, closed the door of the cabin as quietly as he could. The ship was still locked in the ice of the Arctic. This past week the sun had been dipping ever closer to the horizon, and it couldn't be long before the six-month night began. He hoped beyond all hope that the ice would release them before that happened. His crew had shot a few seals and even a polar bear, but despite this there was still far from enough food to sustain them through the winter months.

During his spare time he had listened to Victor Frankenstein's story, and had simultaneously watched the man drifting ever closer to his death. Victor couldn't be more than twenty-five – although Walton guessed he might be younger. The man had been so delirious throughout much of his account that it was impossible to tell either his age or the truth of his tale. How much of it did the captain believe? He didn't know. The giant figure he'd seen on the ice made him think there might be some truth in Victor's story. But all logical sense persuaded him that the rambling account was just the raving of a very sick man.

That Victor was dying was, however, certain. The *Margaret Saville* had only a limited stock of medicines, and none had proved useful against the fever that he was suffering from. Walton punched the side of his fist against the bulkhead. During the past week he had come to like and admire Victor. To be sure, the young man had done some very stupid things – if his tale was to be credited – but his aim had always been to help humanity. He had wanted to create a better humanity.

Captain Walton found Rostop on deck.

"He's dying." said Walton wearily.

"Could have told you that when he came on board," said Rostop, bluntly.

"When I left him he was falling asleep. He told me how he followed this creature of his up through the northern lands. He said that the monster seemed to want him to catch up with it – that it left clues to help him find it."

"That's if there ever was a monster," said Rostop.

"I think there was," said Captain Walton. "Whether it was a real monster or just a projection of Victor's mind I couldn't tell you, but he certainly believes in it. It was real to him – and, remember, we saw that giant creature on the sled."

"We saw a big man," said Rostop, tersely.

"A very big man. Too big to be a man, I think."

Rostop took a pipe from his pocket. "Think we'll get out of this?" he said, gesturing at the waste.

"Maybe," said Walton. "If God is with us."

There was a loud groan from below. For an instant Walton thought it was Victor. Then the boat swayed.

"God does seem to be with us," he said, keeping his voice as cool as possible.

There was another lurch. The timbers creaked. The sailors, who were returning from a hunting trip, began to cheer – and to run over to the ship, because cracks were starting to open up in the ice.

"We're going to be free!" said Walton. He punched Rostop affectionately on the shoulder. "Didn't I tell you?"

The first mate grinned. "No, but I'll say to the crew you did."

"Bring out some rum. Quickly, so it's ready when they come aboard."

Chuckling, Walton turned to go to his cabin. Then he remembered Victor. He supposed he should look in on him. Perhaps a little rum would revive the man. He tapped at the door of Victor's cabin. There was no response. Then a tremendous shock hit the *Margaret Saville*. Walton instinctively glanced up, as if the ship had been struck by a thunderbolt. He smiled to himself. Not a thunderbolt at all: more of the ice was breaking up around the hull.

Through the cabin door, he heard a noise. He tapped again. Still there was no reply. There was a sound, though. He put his ear to the wood and listened more closely. Someone – Walton could hardly believe it was Victor – was sobbing hoarsely. The captain grabbed the handle and threw open the door. A huge figure was crouched over the man Walton had come to call a friend. It turned its face toward him, its eyes filled with hatred. His stomach lurched.

"You!" Walton hissed. "So Victor was telling the truth!"

"Yes, me," said the creature. Its face was repulsive. No wonder, Walton thought, that everyone rejected it on sight.

"I came to ask him for forgiveness," said the creature, "but he was dead before I could."

"You killed him? "

"No. He was already dead. He was my father and my mother, and he treated me cruelly – abandoning me when I was hardly born – but at last, out there on the ice, I discovered that I loved him. When I saw the pack-ice splintering I decided I must come to him to beg forgiveness for all the terrible crimes I've committed against him. But he was dead."

"You've committed a crime against my ship," said the captain. "You've torn a hole through her side to reach here."

"It's nothing you can't repair. Look at Frankenstein instead. He's past any mending you could do."

Walton looked at the frail figure sprawled on the bunk. Maybe it was better this way. Who would want to live with the memories of a wife and a younger brother and a friend murdered, and of a father dying of grief, and of another friend hanged unjustly?

Victor, through his arrogance, had brought many of his sufferings upon himself – and, more than that, upon those around him – but he had never meant to do any harm.

"Do you repent all the things you've done?" said Walton, wondering where his courage came from.

"I can't repent," said the creature, moving back to the hole it had made in the *Margaret Saville*'s side. "I don't have the capacity to feel repentance, or remorse, or guilt. Frankenstein built me as best he could, so that I had the form of a man. If his experiment hadn't been interrupted, I'd have been so like a man that you wouldn't have been able to tell the difference.

"But what he wasn't able to do was to give me a soul. I've no real conscience. I can tell right from wrong, but I can't really understand why I should do one rather than the other. Except now . . . now I've learned a little about the world and, sitting out on the ice, letting my hatred ebb, about myself."

"I can take you back with us," said Walton, moving cautiously into the cabin.

"I wouldn't want you to. I'm always going to be an exile from the human race. Somewhere out there on the ice I'll die, eventually – I have no idea how long my allotted lifespan might be. But I do want to die, alone, unmocked – unmocked by those who were given an easier life than I was."

"I wouldn't mock you," said Walton, quietly. "You've done awful things, but it's easy to see why you have. I wouldn't –"

"And the rest of the world? Your crew?" The creature snarled viciously. "Captain, I'm not safe in human company. I tell you, I have no ability to tell the difference between good and evil. I couldn't trust myself – so why should anyone else trust me? If I weren't hanged for my crimes I'd be caged away as a freak, perhaps displayed for the fascination of pretty women brought to see me by the men who wanted to impress them." The creature was spitting the words. It understood only too well.

"No, I don't want to come back to civilization with you. Civilization threw sticks and stones at me, just because I was ugly. Civilization would do the same again. Much better for me to find my death in the ice. The cold will kill me, in the end, but at least it will not deliberately torment me."

More swiftly than Walton's eyes could follow, the creature sprang out through the hole it had beaten in the ship's side. The captain took a few paces forward. Through the breach he watched the monster leap from one ice floe to the next until it reached the pack-ice.

Moments later it was lost in darkness and distance.

OTHER VERSIONS OF THE FRANKENSTEIN STORY

Almost immediately after its publication, *Frankenstein* was adapted and retold by other writers. Even today, almost two centuries later, it continues to inspire new versions in various forms: theatre, films, comics, and even music, as well as books. Some of the most famous of these are listed below.

Theatre The first play to use the story was Brinsley Peake's *Presumption: or the Fate of Frankenstein* (1823). Mary Shelley herself went to see it, but was unimpressed; like many other adaptations, it concentrated on the horror element and ignored the book's scientific and philosophical arguments. Three years later, Henry Milner's *Frankenstein or the Man and the Monster* was the first version that actually showed the animation of the monster on stage.

Films The first Frankenstein film was made in 1910, by J. Searle Dawley, and lasted only twelve minutes. It contained the first representation of the monster on film. Over the next 20 years many films dealing with the creation of artificial life were made in the USA, Italy and Germany. Some of them retold parts of the Frankenstein story; others reinvented the idea.

In Fritz Lang's *Metropolis* (1926), a mad scientist invents a female monster. This film provided a lot of the visual imagery that is now associated with later Frankenstein films. The most important of these, simply called *Frankenstein*, was directed by James Whale in 1931 for Universal Studios. Many critics claim that this is the best horror film ever made, and it is this version of the monster that most people think of when they think of *Frankenstein* – the beast with a flat head and bolts through its neck. In this film, the monster was played by the actor Boris Karloff. This portrayal was so successful that many people now think that "Frankenstein" is the name of the monster, not its creator.

In 1957 the British film company Hammer made *The Curse of Frankenstein*. While many of the characters in the book remain the same, the story is retold and, if anything, is more violent and horrific than the original. This was the first in Hammer's series of Frankenstein films which continued for nearly 20 years.

Young Frankenstein, by Mel Brooks, was released in 1974. It uses the story as the basis for the first Frankenstein comedy, but it is also a very clever spoof of older Frankenstein films. It is also the only Frankenstein film which has a happy ending – the monster gets married and becomes an accepted member of society.

Comics In the early 1970s Marvel, the American comic publisher, published a series of 18 books called *The Frankenstein Monster*. These are now very rare collectors' items.

Music *The Rocky Horror Show* (1973), written by Richard O'Brien, is a parody of the Frankenstein story retold as a rock musical. Part comedy, part horror, it was also filmed in 1975 as *The Rocky Horror Picture Show*.

In the 1970s and 1980s, the funk musician George Clinton released a number of albums about Dr Funkenstein, a space alien who created a race of funk monsters dedicated to filling the world with dance music. *The Clones of Dr Funkenstein* (1976), by Clinton's band Parliament, is among the best-known of these.

Frankenstein!! (1977), by the Austrian composer HK Gruber, is a musical entertainment for a singer and group of musicians. It is based on a number of rhymes written for children by the poet H.C. Artmann. Some of these are based on the Frankenstein story. Others are about different characters from horror, cowboy and spy films.

Another Usborne Classic

from the story by

BRAM STOKER

When the other passengers on the
stagecoach found out where Jonathan was
going, they stared at him in astonishment.
Then they started whispering in
Transylvanian and Jonathan heard some
words that he knew: *pokol* and *vrolok*. The
first word meant hell, and the second . . .
Jonathan shivered. It meant vampire.

When Jonathan Harker arrives at creepy Castle
Dracula in Transylvania, he has no idea what to
expect, but all too soon his host's horrible nocturnal
habits have him fearing for his life. . . This is the story
of a battle against the forces of evil, as the eccentric
Professor Van Helsing and his brave young friends
take on the vilest vampire in the world.